W9-CDW-865

Praise for Juli Zeh

"Zeh challenges readers to consider how complicit we are in our current political dilemmas."
Los Angeles Times

•

Praise for New Year

"Because the thriller and the analysis of society are here so densely intertwined, *New Year* is perhaps Juli Zeh's best book to date."
Süddeutsche Zeitung

"*New Year* is an impressively original book whose elegant construction testifies to Zeh's writerly prowess."
New Books in German

"Past experience is part of us, like a code in computer software—Zeh, in her usual straight-forward way, has condensed this to make a compact novel."
Stern

"A thrilling, cinematic story."
VPRO Boeken

"With *New Year*, Juli Zeh has succeeded in writing a lost-memory thriller and at the same time an accurate psychogram of today's overwhelmed fathers."
WDR 3

"With *New Year*, Juli Zeh shows that good enter-tainment can indeed be easily coupled with depth and literary quality. This psycho-thriller is well on its way to becoming a bestseller."
SRF 2 Kultur

"A compact, highly concentrated story with gripping dynamics and a superb 'aha' effect."
SWR2

"Juli Zeh has written not only an enthralling psychogram of a man, but also quite nearly a classical tragedy."
Südwest Presse

"*New Year* dives deep into the psyche of modern, emancipated man and investigates to what extent

experiences in our childhood influence how we live our lives as adults."
JAN

"This book develops into a rapid, exciting drama, of a kind you might have never read before."
Der Kleinborsteler

"Juli Zeh maintains suspense, homes in on the moments of unreality, the sense of magic, and offers an unexpected twist at the end."
Libération

"The landscape is a metaphor, the natural elements an allegory of the main character's inner turmoil and traumas by means of which the reader, witness to a progressive, gripping psychological unveiling left unresolved until the final page, sees this hidden inner world resurface."
Diacritik

"*New Year* explores the profundities of being and attempts a decryption of the mechanisms of the unconscious, all the while following the codes of the thriller to ensnare the reader. Juli Zeh

successfully constructs a psychological novel, all the while avoiding the pitfalls of the genre. This hypnotically written novel is one you devour."
La Provence

"An intense and gripping psychological thriller. The second part of this novel, impressive in its mastery of narrative, will cost you some hours of sleep."
Midi Libre

"Juli Zeh marvelously describes the traumatism of abandonment. Reaching the summit is an effective allegory for Henning's dive into himself. The German novelist brilliantly succeeds in launching him into the depths of himself and of what he left unsaid, all the better to liberate him of it."
L'Alsace

"Juli Zeh wields the mechanisms of the psychological thriller and adds her own trademark, which is to let the heroes brush with catastrophe without always drowning in it. The tension the novelist keeps going isn't resolved until the final page. *New Year* manages to open up the silent depths of lives that are too plotted out, much like

the potholes that shake up rental cars on the
roads of the Canary Islands."
Le Monde des Livres

"Juli Zeh dramatizes the resurgence of that which
has been suppressed by means of an efficient
thriller that leaves the reader breathless and
deeply shaken."
L'Obs

"The suppressed drama suddenly unravels before
our bewildered eyes, leaving our hearts pounding
and our minds racing. Once devoured, *New Year*
obsesses its reader for days on end. Juli Zeh
strikes hard and strikes home."
Transfuge

"An experience of psychological dissection.
New Year is a vertiginous plunge into the psyche
of a man straining under the weight of what he
believes he must achieve and, in a subtle game of
smoke and mirrors, into our own neuroses. With
the tale of a mad ascent, the novel defuses, with
the author's characteristic scathing and elegant
irony, the diktat of perfection and permanence
extolled by the media that has invaded the sphere

of social life and intimacy, and invites us to respond with a middle finger stuck up with pride."
Lire

"You don't know where you're going, but you unconsciously feel that you are going far, very far away, a lot farther than the Lanzarote roads. To tell you more would be to spoil the pleasure provided by this novel, which is as brilliant and amoral as can be and explores our most common depths."
Page des libraires

"It is genuinely admirable how, page after page, Juli Zeh manages to develop a truly nerve-racking thriller. Ever changing register, she always starts with questions rising from the conditions of life in today's society."
DNA

"Juli Zeh adapts adult distress to children's terrors, joins a faltering present with a foundering past. As always in her novels, she shows a formidable mastery of time. *New Year* is an intimate drama, as well as a promise."
Julieamimots.com

"With total mastery of these fine mechanics, Juli Zeh confronts a man with his demons."
ALEXANDRE FILLON, *Les Echos Week-End*

"Juli Zeh has rediscovered the somewhat lost art of the psychological thriller."
Libération

"In *New Year*, Juli Zeh invents a new type: the hysterical man. She could just as easily have written two separate books. A poignant sketch of modern narcissistic parents, and their roots in the past."
Trouw

•

Praise for Eagles and Angels

"Folding the story of Max's tortured love for both women into a larger chronicle of European drug smuggling and related war crimes, Zeh weaves a nightmarishly effective tale of personal and societal collapse."
Publishers Weekly

"Zeh's style is always enjoyable. She writes brittle little sentences, trying to shock and often succeeding. Her characters are vivacious and thrilling; she tussles with big themes, and is fuelled by an admirable fury. What shines through is Zeh's exhilarating ambition, as she dares to plunge deep into the dark heart of Europe and expose its core."
The Guardian

•

Praise for Empty Hearts

"*Empty Hearts* has the veneer of a thriller but it's more accurate to call it a chiller: chilling in the accuracy of its satire and chilling in its diagnosis of our modern malaise."
New York Times

"Darkly entertaining. A thoughtful political thriller with a provocative sense of humor."
Kirkus Reviews, starred review

"Will keep readers turning the pages. Zeh makes it easy to suspend disbelief in this cold-blooded and macabre future."
Publishers Weekly

"*Empty Hearts* explores interesting ideas about the price of failure to act against tyranny and the moral complicity of people who capitalize on a bad situation, or do nothing in the hopes that it will all go away."
Los Angeles Times

"2019 has seen a string of novelists exploring the destabilized Western political psyche, but *Empty Hearts* strikes me as one of the strongest so far. It asks, what if the current political climate led not to catastrophe, but to stagnation? Its answer comes in the form of both a riveting thriller and a nuanced piece of social science fiction—predictive and precautionary. Brilliantly executed—one of the standouts of the year."
New Scientist

"A gripping, character-driven thriller that's rooted in insightful political commentary—perfect for beach reading and book groups."
Booklist

•

Praise for Dark Matter

"A thrilling read as well as a terrific mental workout."
The Guardian

"A clever and truly entertaining read."
The Independent

"Zeh constructs an impressive matrix of information for each of her key players and provides descriptions that are vivid and original. Her often unexpected imagery is precise and pithy—this philosophical thriller is well paced; one turns the pages impatient for the denouement."
Times Literary Supplement

"Juli Zeh's new novel *Dark Matter* combines crime novel, love story, and physical speculation."
Die Tageszeitung

"A compelling novel, thrilling yet profound. This book makes for a wonderful read, gripping until the last page. A masterpiece!"
Financial Times Deutschland

Praise for Decompression

"Zeh's award-winning thriller climaxes with a scene of splendid drama."
The Guardian

"Deftly translated by John Cullen, Zeh plays with our expectations throughout. Like *The Method*, this is a story about obsession—this time with status, looks, and celebrity culture."
The Independent

"Erotic intrigue, deep-sea diving and clients from hell make for a lively mix—the gathering suspense is complemented by nuanced characterization in a pleasingly unpredictable work."
Kirkus Reviews

"A mesmerizing and disturbing psychological thriller. Zeh's talent pulls this morally murky tale up from the depths and toward a redeeming light."
Wall Street Journal

"A deft thriller."
Publishers Weekly

"Gripping ... Zeh is exceptional at building tension, and her use of shifting viewpoints keeps the reader guessing to the end. A darkly comic thriller that is impossible to put down."
Library Journal

"A tale that unfolds at a high level of psychological excitement."
Der Spiegel

"A nightmarish, furious, cold thriller. Juli Zeh is at her literary best when she's describing underwater silence, when she's describing situations in which isolation is total and the world as it exists above water is bidden farewell. This is phenomenal."
Frankfurter Allgemeine Sonntagszeitung

"Juli Zeh's love-triangle drama easily bears comparison with the work of Patricia Highsmith, doyenne of the conspicuously amoral."
Brigitte

●

Praise for The Method

"This is a brilliant, disturbing and wildly imaginative picture of the nanny state run mad; how far should the State be allowed to poke its nose into a citizen's business?"
The Times

"Zeh seems to have won every European literary prize going. Three years since its first publication in German (it is translated here with tremendous gusto by Sally-Ann Spencer), Zeh's novel is even more relevant to our over-structured, over-quantified times."
The Guardian

"An impressively plausible account of a conformist society disguised as a utopia."
The Independent

"In Sally-Ann Spencer's superb translation from the German, Juli Zeh's novel gives form to a dystopia that remains hauntingly recognizable."
Times Literary Supplement

"Thoughtful and intelligent—Zeh's main character Mia is an intellectual heroine as much as a physical rebel."
Sunday Herald

•

Praise for In Free Fall

"A gripping, high-toned philosophical thriller. Readers who can surrender to Zeh's radical rewriting of the rules of detective fiction and the physical universe will find it revelatory."
Kirkus Reviews

"Erudite digressions and vivid characters—such as a detective with a trusting nature who learns always 'to assume the opposite of what she was thinking'—combine with a devastating 11th-hour reveal to make a memorable intellectual thriller."
Publishers Weekly

"An elegant quasi-thriller about physics, murder, and the solving of murders. This is one of the best books of the year. Zeh has enough control to keep the murder from being lurid and the

physics from being dull. Her prose is sharp and often witty, and the excellent translation means every moment shines brightly."
New York Observer

"A highly cinematic thriller. Zeh's smart novel will appeal to a wide range of readers."
Library Journal

"Add a hospital scandal and two of the quirkiest detectives in fiction, mix with Juli Zeh's thrumming, moody prose, and you have one of the finest crime novels you'll read."
Herald Sun

"It is such a delight to watch Juli Zeh play her entire repertoire of literary skill, challenging the conventions of the classical detective story with subtle irony."
Die Zeit

"A masterfully constructed story of an intense friendship between two physicists, a marriage, a kidnapping, and a murder, *In Free Fall* plunges the reader into a hyper-reality that is as seductive as it is disturbing."
Boston Globe

"Give me a crime novel of ideas, where two physics professors, friends, and rivals, opposites but startlingly similar, do emotional battle on an intellectual canvas, raise the stakes through betrayal, the possible kidnapping of a child, and embroil a romantic-leaning police detective in the complicated machinations of quantum theory, and holy hell, I think I have myself one of my favorite books of the year."
Los Angeles Times

"The most intellectually satisfying thriller you'll read this summer. Slyly intelligent and enigmatic. The brainiac's beach read."
Daily Beast

"*In Free Fall* is very clever, and often astounding. A wonderful exhibition of bravura novel writing."
Curled Up With A Good Book

"A novel from Juli Zeh's pen is always an adventure, because each of them opens up an entirely new world. This is Juli Zeh's unique talent: her sharp intellect absorbs the most complex issues, including elementary particles, to then put them into words with such playful precision it makes

you swoon. *In Free Fall* takes the bird's-eye view, unorthodox, nerve-racking, simply unforget-table—like Hitchcock's masterpiece."
Brigitte

"*In Free Fall* is the virtuosic presentation of an amazing narration. Juli Zeh steers through with confidence and ease."
Welt am Sonntag

New Year

Juli Zeh
New Year

Translated from the German
by Alta L. Price

WORLD EDITIONS
New York, London, Amsterdam

Published in the USA in 2021 by World Editions LLC, New York
Published in the UK in 2021 by World Editions Ltd., London

World Editions
New York | London | Amsterdam

Printed by Lake Book, USA

Library of Congress Cataloging in Publication Data is available

ISBN 978-1-64286-099-3

First published as *Neujahr* in Germany in 2019 by Luchterhand
Literaturverlag.

The translation of this work was supported by a grant from the
Goethe-Institut.

Twitter: @WorldEdBooks
Facebook: @WorldEditionsInternationalPublishing
Instagram: @WorldEdBooks
YouTube: World Editions
www.worldeditions.org

Book Club Discussion Guides are available on our website.

For David, who knows what this is about.

HIS LEGS HURT. In back, where there are muscles one rarely uses with names he's forgotten. With each push of the pedal his toes come up against the lining of his shoes— sneakers meant for jogging, not cycling. Henning's cheap cycling shorts don't fully protect him from chafing, he has no water, and the bike is far too heavy.

But the temperature is almost perfect. The sun hangs white in the sky, but doesn't burn. If Henning were on a lounger sheltered from the wind, he'd be warm. If he were walking along the seashore, he'd need a jacket.

Cycling is pure relaxation. The bike gives him time to himself, and riding helps him unwind. It's a little break between work and family. The kids are two and four.

The wind keeps him from breaking a

sweat. The wind is strong today, a bit too strong. Theresa began complaining at breakfast, she loves to complain about the weather, and doesn't really mean it, but it bothers him anyway. Too warm, too cold, too humid, too dry. Today, too windy. You couldn't take the kids outside. They'd have to stay inside all day, rather than heading out into the sun. Henning was the one who'd insisted on this vacation, anyway. They could've celebrated Christmas at home, in their spacious apartment in Göttingen, saving money and sparing themselves the stress. They could've gone to visit friends or rented a place nearby. But then Henning up and decided they'd head to Lanzarote. Night after night he surfed the web, looking through images of white seafoam on black beaches, of palms and volcanos and a landscape that resembled the interior of a stalactite cave. He pored over charts showing average temperatures and forwarded his findings to Theresa. But mostly he clicked through countless images of whitewashed villas for rent. One after the other, night after night, until late. He'd plan to stop at a certain point and go to bed, but then he'd click on the next listing. He'd devour each image, voracious as an addict, almost as if he were looking for a specific house.

And now here they were, all these villas, set far back from the road, spaciously scattered across the campo. From afar they looked like white bits of lichen growing on the dark ground. From a middle distance they appeared to have been arrayed according to size. Only when slowly riding by could you fully make them out: impressive haciendas, often high up in the terraced hills, surrounded by whitewashed walls with wrought-iron gates. The main buildings were set amid ornate, overgrown gardens with tall palms, contorted cacti, and exuberant bougainvillea. Mostly rental cars in the driveways. Various patios pointed in various directions. Surrounded by panoramas, overlooks, and the horizon line. Volcanic mountains, sea, and sky. Riding by, Henning took it all in with eager eyes. He imagined how it must feel to live there. The sheer joy, the sense of success, the grandeur.

Without asking Theresa, he finally booked

a place for himself and the family, two weeks in the sun, over Christmas and New Year's. Not a villa, but something within their budget. A skinny slice of a townhouse sandwiched between others that all looked alike, each with a patio protected from the wind and a teensy yard. Very pretty, but very small. The shared pool is turquoise blue and well tended. The water is usually too cold for a swim.

Back in Germany it's sleeting and one degree above freezing, he'd replied to Theresa's moaning and groaning this morning.

New year, new you, he silently chants to himself with each stroke of the pedal. The wind is strong and blows straight into his face. The road starts to ascend, Henning slowly makes headway. He rented the wrong bike, the tires are too thick, the frame too heavy. But it gives him more time to take in the houses. He knows what each one looks like inside; the online images have stuck in his mind. Tile floors and open hearths. Bathrooms with natural stone walls. Double beds draped in flowing mosquito nets. Enclosed patios with a palm tree growing in the middle. Ocean view out front, mountain view out back. Four bedrooms, three bathrooms. A smiling wife in light linen pants and a billowy blouse. Happy kids calmly at play, keeping themselves entertained. A strong man, responsible and affectionate with his family, but independent at heart and always in control. This man reclines on a deck chair, enjoying his first cocktail of the day in the early afternoon. Robust walls, small windows.

Renting a place like that would have cost €1,800 a week. The apartment costs €60 a night. They have a bedroom with a four-foot-six bed, which is a bit narrow for Henning. There's another room with a child's bed and crib, and even a fully stocked changing table, complete with wet wipes, baby oil, and a small supply of diapers. The living room shelves are stocked with thrillers left behind by previous guests, most in English, a few in German. The kitchen is open, and a sliding glass door leads to the outdoor dining area. The yard has a grill and built-in benches where they sit and drink wine after the kids have gone to bed. Young people are staying in the neighboring apartment on one side, but they're out all day and only come back to sleep. On the other side is a British couple over sixty who are as quiet as Henning and Theresa, and so far they haven't complained about the kids.

We really lucked out. The place has been great. Bibbi's slept like a log since the very first night, better than at home even, Henning and Theresa repeatedly remark. They keep reassuring one another it's a charming place, and it really is. The weather's been perfect, aside from the wind, which only picked up this morning. They've already been to the beach a few times. Meanwhile, Theresa has agreed it was a good idea to come. At first she was against it. Henning had hoped to make it a pleasant surprise for her by booking it in secret, thinking that would convince her. So she wasn't reproachful, that's not her style. Instead, she silently conveys the impression he's messed up. Why the Canary Islands? Too stressful, too expensive, too far out. Theresa isn't usually one to change her mind. But now she's glad they're here, the wind is the only thing she can't stand.

The rental car costs €135 per week, the bike €28 per day. On their first grocery trip to the EUROSPAR they spent over €300. If they eat out, the tab for two kids and two adults, including one drink per person, ranges from €30 to €50. The flight was cheap, but Henning still finds it outrageous that kids' tickets are almost the same price as adults'. He doesn't know why he always pays such close attention to what everything costs. They aren't exactly on the breadline. But there's a calculator in Henning's head that Theresa would find laughable if she knew about it. He can't help it. He always takes note of what things are worth—or, more precisely, their price. Maybe money is the last organizing system left in this world.

New year, new you.

Aside from him there are hardly any other cyclists out. More precisely, Henning hasn't yet spotted a single one. Maybe the wind is keeping them home. Or they're just sleeping it off. Men who don't have kids. Or who manage it better than he does.

At the bike shop they asked him what kind of riding he planned to do. Just ride around a bit, Henning replied. The man recommended a lean mountain bike, medium tread, with air shocks. That way you can even cruise down some of the sandy trails, he said.

Back home Henning no longer trains regularly, he just can't get round to it. He used to ride every weekend, sometimes more than one hundred kilometers a day. Lanzarote, the cycling paradise. That's what it's called on the Internet. Good roads, steep slopes. All the pros train here. Henning figures it's a good idea to try out one of the many routes while on vacation, not too long, and at a relaxed pace. They've been here for a week already, and he hasn't gotten on the bike even once. Until today.

It was a spontaneous idea. After breakfast he stepped outside and looked up at Mount Atalaya, a dark, dormant volcano overlooking the Atlantic. And Henning knew he had to climb it. The village of Femés stands 500 meters above sea level. The road there is a wide, winding ribbon, climbing evenly and gently until the steep bit at the very end. It didn't look far. Henning called back into the house, "I'm going for a little ride, be back soon, bye," and closed the door without waiting for an answer.

New year, new you. What's great about cycling is that all you need to do is pedal. That's it. It's going well. Slowly, but well. Aside from his hamstrings, Henning feels absolutely fit.

It's hard to believe they've only been on the island for a week. Henning feels like Christmas was a long time ago already. Christmas Eve was quite nice, somehow. Although for four years now "nice" has meant "fun for the kids." Theresa insisted on getting a Christmas tree. Right after they arrived, she drove their rental car around for hours, on an island without any vegetation worth mentioning, in order to get hold of a spruce tree. All the while, Henning sat around in the house they'd rented with Jonas and Bibbi, discovering just how stressful vacation with the kids is when you haven't brought along the Legos, toy train set, or stuffed animal collection.

In Henning's worldview, there are kids who'd be entirely satisfied with a little yard like the one here. They'd spend hours playing in the black gravel that covers the entire space in place of grass. But Bibbi and Jonas don't. Sometimes Henning wonders if they're doing something wrong. Jonas's favorite question is "What do we do now?" and even Bibbi already says "I'm bored," a phrase she learned from her brother.

Theresa thinks they're just too young to keep themselves occupied yet. All the kids that age in their circle of acquaintances need a play schedule. But Henning wants to be a father, not an entertainer or playmate. He thinks there's something off about the very notion. When he was little, it would never have even occurred to him or his sister to ask their mother to play with them. It's hard to understand what's changed since then.

Theresa finally realized that there were no Christmas trees on the entire island, or rather, more precisely, only very few available on preorder through a garden shop catering to German expats, which were then imported by ship. So she came back with a little pre-decorated plastic Christmas tree she kept hidden in the trunk so she could tell the kids Santa Claus had brought it. Ever since Bibbi and Jonas were born, she's put this show on every year, secretively summoning gifts from Santa Claus. Even if they were smack in the middle of the Himalayas she'd find a way to get a Christmas tree and hide it from the kids until showtime. Henning is often annoyed by her dogged determination, although deep down he knows he's just jealous. For one, because Theresa fights until she gets what she wants. For another, because she also had Christmas trees brought to her by Santa Claus when she was little. Her first peek at the tree aglow with candles and decked in glass ball ornaments in the living room is one of Theresa's most cherished childhood memories.

Henning and Luna usually had no tree at all. When they did, it was the best their mother could find during her stressed-out errands, usually the smallest, most stunted little one, which she'd stuff into her already overstuffed trunk. Aside from never having time, their mother never had money either. Their father had left when Henning was Jonas's age, four or five. When Henning thinks back to his childhood, he sees his mother, Luna, and himself. His father Werner isn't in the picture. He has no memory of the time before Werner "started a new life," as his mother puts it.

After all, he's heard it isn't unusual for people's earliest memories to date back to age five or six. At the publishing house, he once worked on a book about human memory. It said that most early memories actually come from photos or family stories. You could even fabricate them, by showing adults manipulated photos from their past. Then they'd remember things that never really happened.

Henning finds that rather eerie. He'd rather have no memories at all. But there actually are a few photos of all four of them as a family: his beautiful mother, blond Henning, Werner beaming with a smile beneath his black mustache, and between them little Luna with a big gap-toothed grin, looking adorably naughty. But Henning neither recognizes his father in that mustachioed image of Werner nor remembers how Luna lost both her incisors at such a young age, even though he's heard the story about the tricycle accident a million times.

And unlike Theresa's Christmas trees, the ones his mother got never had anything to do with Santa Claus. Instead, they were so-you'll-finally-shut-up trees. Henning and Luna loved them despite, or maybe because of, their bent little branches. But Henning doesn't even want to think about that; if it were up to him, he'd never lay eyes on another Christmas tree for the rest of his life.

But when Christmas Eve came to their holiday rental he was actually grateful Theresa had been so persistent. The kids stood rapt before the cheaply decorated little plastic tree, staring wide-eyed at the string of lights, poking at the ornaments with their fingers. Jonas liked the snowmen in pirate bandanas hanging from the fake twigs, and Bibbi liked the little birds in woolly caps. Henning stood nearby, wondering whether one day at least Jonas would remember this moment. Whether any detail whatsoever of this trip would stick with him.

The mountain's surface has wrinkles inhabited by shadow. Almost as if night had retreated there, awaiting its regular evening deployment. Around six each afternoon the darkness rises from these gullies and swiftly envelops the entire island. By day the view is crystal clear, the mountains' contours are sharp, and the colors are so intense they look photoshopped. Henning feels unreal amid this lichen-spotted moonscape; neither his bike nor he himself belong here. He's read about the most recent eruptions here, 300-odd years ago, in the guidebook. How Mount Timanfaya covered a third of the island in fresh lava flow. How it wiped out flora and fauna, and covered entire swaths of land in ash and scoria. Toxic vapor, saltwater geysers, igneous rock hurled all about. It left behind a kind of geological zero hour, dawn on earth. A mineralogical fresh start, faceless, historyless, mute.

The guidebook says some people hate Lanzarote while others adore it. Henning isn't yet sure which camp he falls into.

These are the very first moments he's had to himself, just him and the island. Up to now the days have been determined by the kids: playground, beach, pirate museum, camel rides. Ice cream, go-karts, zoo, another ice cream. Who could stand spending the entire day home with two little kids, any-way? With kids, vacation is a more stressful version of everyday life. Parents can't get a moment's rest, and try with all their might to act as bastions against chaos, boredom, and mood swings. They read the chapter "For Families" in the guidebook, scour the super-market shelves for a specific kind of sausage, and gravitate toward children's channels on TV. They learn how to collapse a stroller and fit it into the far-too-small rental car trunk, wage battle with the straps of the car seat, and enthuse over how kid-friendly Spaniards are, how all the restaurants have IKEA high chairs at the ready, how there's a remarkable number of dads at every playground. They've long known that work is no longer the enemy of free time, but rather a self-defense strategy for escaping the kids' clutches. Only once they're back at work will they have time to recover from vacation.

"It's just a phase," that's one of Theresa's catchphrases. Sometimes Henning hears, "It's just a phrase." It's bad enough that both are true.

So in order to celebrate New Year's Eve

in family-friendly style, they booked a last-minute prix-fixe dinner at a hotel called Las Olas. The first shift, which started at 6:00 p.m., included four courses, and ended at 8:30 p.m., since the next shift started at 9:00 p.m. It was a humiliating prospect, but was best for the kids' body clocks, which would only be off by a couple of hours this way.

The Las Olas dining room was so vast it looked endless. Eight-person tables were packed one next to the other. It smelled like a cafeteria. They'd expected something a little more festive. At least kids ate free of charge.

Straightaway Theresa sought to make the best of it. Make-the-best-of-it is like a pre-programmed setting she shifts into the moment anything goes awry. She decided to take the kids for a stroll through the lobby, so they could gape at the Swarovski-studded Christmas tree, while Henning found their table and got everything ready. He was to arrange for a high chair, set the wet wipes out, and swap their glasses with plastic cups he brought along.

Stepping into the dining room, Henning felt like he was on a cruise ship, even though he'd never set foot on one. Guests were already seated at most tables, eyeing newcomers with anticipation or studying the menu they'd presumably already memorized. He was uncomfortable sitting down with strangers. In the presence of others, keeping the kids in line became a desperate duty. Henning scanned the tables for number 27 and finally found it, next to a fountain modeled to look like a natural spring flowing into a pool where a couple of koi swam. That would provide at least fifteen minutes' diversion, he estimated. He found the settings somewhat less encouraging, as he'd need to move the various plates, utensils, glasses, and fancily folded napkins to a safe spot beyond the kids' reach. Happily, a high chair was already set up.

On the other side of the table an older couple stood to shake his hand, wishing him Merry Christmas in German and introducing themselves with names he didn't catch. He said his wife and kids would come any minute now, and they said "Wunderbar!" without even a hint of irony.

Henning decided he'd relax. He had every

reason to. Their vacation was going as well as possible, indeed, almost perfectly. Even at the airport, the moment they'd stepped off the plane, he'd felt the particularly bright, airy, light atmosphere. The Spanish were friendly, and even with the kids he felt welcome everywhere. Nobody ever gave you the feeling you were doing something wrong. It was as if the word *stress* had never been invented.

But *it* nevertheless turned up again last night. In the dining room at Las Olas he couldn't have seen *it* coming. As he sat at table 27 waiting for Theresa and the kids, he thought back on an entire week without *it*. A week of normal life, normal sleep, normal troubles, normal joys. It had been the longest disturbance-free time he'd enjoyed in the past two years. Over the last few days he'd repeatedly forbidden himself to even think of *it*, since the mere thought of *it* was capable of luring it out of its cave. Naturally, despite it all, he thought about *it* the whole time. To his amazement, *it* stayed in its den, withdrawn, lying in wait, dormant, or whatever it did when it wasn't tormenting him. He usually forbade himself from taking any joy in *its* absence, too, since even the slightest glimmer of hope led it to strike back even harder. But here, in the overfilled, overheated dining room of Las Olas, he carefully allowed himself just a few moments of joy. And why not? He had it good. He was just a normal guy among normal people. He wasn't going crazy.

The German couple were from Würselen, hometown of Martin Schulz, the current leader of the Social Democratic Party, and went on to say they'd known him since way back when he was a bookseller. Henning nodded and sounded his approval while also keeping an eye out for Theresa and the kids, who he expected would be done with their excursion to admire the Christmas tree any minute now. He finally spotted them a ways off, Theresa stood laughing next to a fully occupied table, where he also saw two kids the same age as Bibbi and Jonas. The four little ones' heads were huddled together, presumably gathered around a toy. Maybe Bibbi was showing off the little squeaking plastic guinea pig she'd gotten for Christmas, which caused a stir everywhere she went. Suddenly Henning was overcome by how much he loved his children—so much that at times it was pure torture.

Theresa lifted a hand to her mouth and let out a laugh so loud Henning heard it all the way across the room. Observing her from a distance, he's sometimes struck by how petite she is, as if he'd never noticed it over the years, or had simply forgotten. Barely five foot two yet so full of life. He couldn't even say whether she's beautiful or merely good-looking. She keeps her brown hair cut short and has a strong, compact figure. Her effect on others is enormous. Everyone seems to see something special in her. Not just men, but even women are drawn to her, and apt to start telling her their life stories. What Henning loves most about her is her contagious laugh, even when he's often the one she's laughing at. Her cheeks have recently started to sag a little, but it's so slight that nobody who hasn't known her forever even notices. Henning takes this as a sign that, despite her broad hips, she'll grow gaunter with age, rather than plumper. He doesn't know which he'd prefer. He doesn't like old women in general, but one day he'll be living with one. He likes old men even less, but also knows that someday he'll be one.

With these thoughts *its* feelers begin groping for him, so he rushes to focus his attention on something else. A waiter walks up with a tray full of bubbly. Henning helps himself to one, as do the older couple. He decides their names are Katrin and Karlchen. They offer a toast. He downs his entire glass and immediately feels its effects. He usually doesn't drink much alcohol, especially so early in the evening, and so quickly. He raises a finger to summon the waiter back, and downs a second glass. His surroundings no longer look so chintzy. They were eating an all-inclusive dinner, at an all-inclusive hotel full of all-inclusive-type tourists—so what? Katrin and Karlchen were nice, the décor was tolerable, maybe later there would be a chance to dance, or a magician for the kids. Just as he was thinking Theresa would show up, there she was with the kids. She gave Katrin and Karlchen a warm hello, as if they were old acquaintances. They drank to each other, going straight to the informal *Du*, which was easier and completely the norm on the island. The first course came, scallops, which actually tasted really good, and the kids grabbed a slice of bread and disappeared under the table. Just as he was about to call them back, Theresa put her hand on his arm and said, "Let them."

The evening turned out better than expected. The meal was delicious, and Bibbi and Jonas were scarcely seen. They kept running over to the kids at table 24, with whom they clearly got along well. Theresa periodically went over to fetch them, and each time she'd stay and chat a bit; meanwhile, Henning learned the people at that table were French. Going completely against habit, he'd decided to just stay put, drinking bubbly and waiting for the next course. He enjoyed feeling a little tipsy, and enjoyed the fact that he liked the music Katrin and Karlchen were complaining about, hits from the nineties, "Lemon Tree" and even "Come As You Are"; he could've sung along with them all, and even wanted to.

Katrin and Karlchen were talking politics.

They were the kind of people who followed mainstream media not to gain information, but rather to keep tabs on the prevailing mood, and concurred with the rest of the nation that everything was on the brink of disaster. Still no new national leadership, and on top of that Brexit, Trump, and the radical right-wing AfD. Katrin repeated all the phrases everyone echoed—that something had fundamentally changed, that this was the dawn of a different era, that reality no longer had any role to play in the age of populism and social media. She raised a glass and toasted to 2018 being better than the previous year, and Henning played along even though all the chitchat about things being "post-truth" and "a watershed moment" annoyed him no end.

But Katrin and Karlchen still smiled at the kids, downed their bubbly as fast as Henning, and asked Theresa what she did professionally, whereupon a lively discussion of the best tax tricks ensued.

Over the course of the evening, Henning kept forgetting he wasn't aboard a ship. He pictured the brightly lit room sailing through the placid, pitch-black sea of night. As the clock struck nine and it was time to go, he felt as if midnight had come and gone thrice over. Theresa had spent a lot of time at table 24. Maybe more than at 27. Instead of going to get the kids and coming right back, she'd stayed longer each time, chatting in French, a glass of mineral water in hand.

New year, new you.

Past Playa Blanca the terrain begins to climb, gradually at first. His main battle is against the wind, which is stronger than gravity, comes in gusts that sometimes push him several feet off course, and seems to be trying to force him to turn back. Henning doesn't turn back. As his pulse quickens, he downshifts, adjusts his pace to match the new gear ratio, and concentrates on breathing in sync with each pedal, fully emptying his lungs. One-stroke inhale, two-stroke exhale. It's important to stay calibrated, to avoid running out of breath or getting too sweaty. It's not about speed; he's determined to get to the top, no matter how long it takes. Today is a good day for Femés, he feels well rested despite the lousy night. The first day of the first month, a time virtually made for tackling a challenge. He'll show this New Year what's what.

The past year wasn't good to him. Although by some measures everything was going smoothly, no major illnesses, no deaths, Henning lived with the constant suspicion a catastrophe was about to occur. Meanwhile, *it* had begun pouncing not just at night, but even in broad daylight. Between attacks he wrestled with the dread preceding the next attack. What's more, attacks aside, he hadn't found a balance between work and family. Life felt relentless, he couldn't finish anything and didn't have enough time for anything.

He and Theresa work half days, divvying up childcare and their careers. It's important to them. They took it upon themselves to make this model work with their respective employers, although Theresa's accounting firm was rather more cooperative than the left-leaning nonfiction publishing house where Henning worked. The publisher went so far as to indirectly threaten to fire him, and only gave in when he promised to take work home with him. "A full day's work for a half day's pay," Theresa termed it. But this way he can fully participate in their day-to-day life. "Time management," those are the magic words. He often sits at his manuscript-covered desk in the early-morning or late-night hours, nevertheless worrying he just can't focus as intently on the books as he used to. Luckily none of the authors have complained yet.

The main thing was not to do as their parents did. As a single parent, Henning's mother had worked herself to the bone. And Theresa's mother was solely responsible for the kids while her husband was off at work. So Theresa and Henning agreed from the very start that they wanted something else. Something more contemporary. Fifty-fifty rather than 24/7.

Shortly after Jonas was born the landlord of their three-bedroom apartment in Göttingen renovated the attic of their building, creating six small dorm-style student apartments with a tiny kitchen and a tiny bathroom, plus an extra room that was even smaller, wedged as it was under the sloped roof. Henning and Theresa rent one of these mini-apartments as a home office. Henning likes it up there. The rooms' narrowness, the simple carpeted floors, the empty fridge, the drip coffee machine in the kitchen all remind him of his student days. Of a time when he believed everything would be fine, simply because he'd managed to move away from home.

But Theresa's the one who uses the office most. Because she earns more, Henning feels it's only fair that he takes on more of the housework, and Theresa gives him the impression she expects as much. After mornings at the publishing house, he picks up Bibbi and Jonas from nursery school, cooks lunch, puts his little girl down for a nap, and plays Legos with Jonas for an hour. Then they all go to the playground. When Theresa leaves the home office in the late afternoon, Henning is usually out getting groceries with the kids or has already begun preparing dinner. Sometimes on weekends Theresa offers to take care of the kids for a half day, so he has a few hours to himself. Sometimes he says he should get some work done, but just as often he says it'd be nice for all four of them to do something together. So he packs Bibbi's diaper bag and they all drive off to the nearby nature preserve.

In reality, he's already gotten too used to spending most of his time with the kids. No matter how much they stress him out or get on his nerves, when left alone he no longer knows what to do with himself. There are so many things he hasn't done in so long. Cycling, reading, listening to music, hanging out with friends. But this coming year will be different. From now on he'll ride three days a week, at least three, no matter what else is going on. Theresa will be supportive. She'll be glad he's finally "doing" something again. She always says it's just a matter of time management.

"Doing" is an important word for Theresa. For her, "doing something" is indicative of a successful life. "We need to be doing something again" can mean virtually anything: a shared activity, spring cleaning, vacation planning, having friends over for dinner, visiting family, or reviewing their budget. But to Henning's ear "doing" usually sounds like some kind of threat. His keyword is "functioning." Ultimately, everything in life comes down to whether something functions adequately, and as long as things do, you don't really need to be "doing" anything else.

As a couple, he and Theresa seem to be functioning quite well. Their division of labor within the family functions reasonably well. Henning functions well with the kids, as well as he can, and he's sufficiently functional at work, too, albeit not like he was before. Going forward, cycling will perform the function of reducing his stress levels, something he urgently needs. That's his New Year's resolution. That's why he decided to gradually get back into training, look up suitable cycling routes online, diligently perform warm-up exercises, and stay hydrated throughout each ride. But then over this whole vacation he hasn't managed a single ride, and now it's his first one, on the first day of the first month. High time he showed this New Year he means business.

He'll just have to learn to give up his guilty conscience. Although Theresa's been saying for days that he should finally "do something" with the bike, which was an extra rental on top of the others, one he opted for, he still feels bad leaving her alone with the kids. He knows he owes her. To balance things out again, he'll have to do something more for Theresa, or for the family. But what more can he do, when he's already spending all his free time with the kids? Going forward, by riding three times weekly, he'll be amassing a growing debt, missing hours he won't be able to pay off. He tries telling himself that going for these rides is already balancing the books, since he regularly invests so much more time taking care of the kids and the housework than Theresa does. But that's nonsense; the additional time he spends with the kids is balanced out by Theresa's higher income. It's clear to him that they're even; cycling is an additional line on the ledger.

Lifting his head, Henning sees the Los Ajaches range rise up before him like a brown wall. High up in the saddle between the summit of Atalaya and a hillock named Pico Redondo sit two restaurants along the pass;

they're whitewashed like most buildings on the island, and surrounded by terraces offering panoramic views through a glass wall glinting every now and then in the sunlight. Henning has almost put the entire El Rubicón plain behind him. In a few kilometers the road will enter a canyon. From that point on the route will grow steeper with every push of the pedal. Henning can also see the spot where the road finally hits the rock face. It doubles back on itself in two long switchbacks before rising steeply up to the crest. The cliff looks unreal in the glaring light, like a massive portal shut tight. Like something you'd see in a dream. Like something no one could conquer on a bike.

Henning quickly looks away. The steepest part is still a good way off. He read in the guidebook that many cyclists love this part of the route, so he's sure he can manage it, even if others have trained more and are better equipped than he. In any case, it doesn't help to go crazy worrying in advance. In order to distract himself, Henning concentrates on the white line at the road's edge as his wheels quietly swish along next to it and thinks back again to last night.

The drive home from Las Olas in Puerto del Carmen to their place in Playa Blanca took three-quarters of an hour. In the car the kids sang a song with the words *careless* and *breathless* in the refrain, it had played during dinner. Jonas heard it as *carless* and *brakeless*, which Henning and Theresa found so funny they didn't correct him. They smiled in the dark, and Henning laid his hand on Theresa's thigh as he steered the car through the island night. His bubbly-induced buzz had evaporated, but he still felt a rare degree of freedom, as if cut off from the real world, from everything that weighed him down. It was like he'd found a protective little niche where he could hide from himself. By night the volcanoes looked even more surreal, their silhouettes a deep-black shadow standing out from a light-black sky, as if they were driving through the backdrop of some fantasy film. The moon was behind them, thin as a fingernail clipping; the innumerable stars shone bright. It was the last day of the year, and Henning thought he was happy. He loved his kids, he loved his wife. Even if she'd spent most of the night—New Year's Eve, of all nights—flirting with some French guy at table 24.

Back at the apartment they carried the kids up to bed, went out to the patio, and sat nestled in blankets, since it was getting cold, drinking red wine, since they'd forgotten to buy a bottle of sparkling wine. When Henning's phone rang, Theresa rolled her eyes and went back inside. They both knew it was Luna. It was midnight in Germany, already New Year's, an hour earlier than here. Henning was glad Luna thought of him right at midnight. She was always the first to wish him a happy birthday, too.

"Happy New Year, Big Bro!"

He could hear how drunk she was. She was lisping almost as much as Bibbi, which moved him to tears.

"Happy New Year, Li'l Sis. Where are you?"

Of course she was at a party. Loud music in the background, a hubbub of voices. He heard her occasionally snicker at someone, refusing whatever they'd requested—maybe to dance, or shoot off some fireworks, or a screw.

"In Leipzig, where else? And you guys? How's the weather?"

Henning told her about the weather and warned himself off asking all the questions on the tip of his tongue: Who else is at the party? How you getting home? Where will you sleep tonight? Two minutes later Theresa came back with the wine bottle and gestured that it was time to hang up.

Theresa never could stand Luna. They're the same age, but polar opposites. Theresa has a career, a husband, two kids, and a fully furnished apartment. Luna has none of that; instead, she has an eating disorder and writer's block. Despite all that, Henning sometimes thinks Theresa is jealous of her. There's something mysterious about Luna, something spell-like, as if she bore some dark secret deep within. She's tall, with long, dark tresses that always look a little shaggy, and has a voice that transforms every encounter into a movie scene.

Luna wants to be a writer, and tells everyone so. To hear her talk about her stories, they sound marvelous, like modern-day fairy tales, gloomy and beguiling, with tragic characters and surprising plot twists. Unfortunately she doesn't get much down on paper. But Henning still absolutely believes in her talent. Luna always knows what others are thinking, and often knows what will happen next. She's always switching boyfriends. She switches apartments and cities. She'll hold down a job until she can no longer stand how the work is keeping her from writing, and then she'll try writing again until she's flat broke and convinced she'll never be a real writer. They call one another often. Luna tells Henning what a disaster her life is, he says she should take better care of herself. She frequently asks him for a place to crash, or money. Since they have a home office, every now and then he can offer her refuge for a few days.

Every time Luna needs help Theresa is strictly opposed to the idea. She can complain about Luna for hours on end. Luna isn't a tragic figure, she's just lazy and irresponsible. Like a little girl, she always expects the world to take care of her. And she still gets away with it! While people like Theresa herself go to great lengths to fulfill their responsibilities, Luna chooses to play the fairy-tale princess. She shouldn't make such a fuss about everything. Shouldn't live off of others. Should just grow up once and for all.

When going on about Luna, Theresa stares furiously at Henning, as if he were somehow responsible for her state. He, too, wishes she could be different. But she isn't. And he always gets his way, she crashes in their office for a bit. Luna is the only point of contention where he puts his foot down with Theresa.

"I get it," Luna is quick to say when he tells her of Theresa's disapproval. "Think about it a sec. You and me. When it comes to us two, she's the outsider."

Of course Henning knows what she means. You and me. It's a pact, an oath. Their mother was always busy. She kept food on the table and a roof over their heads. But she didn't have the energy for anything more. Henning took care of his little sister. They were a team, from day one.

"I gotta go," Henning said into the phone.

Theresa was standing next to him on the patio. She'd filled both wineglasses to the brim, and was staring off into the darkness.

"Me too," said Luna. The voices in the background grew louder, and once again someone called her name. "I'll call you. I might have to crash at your place for a few days."

"Take care, Li'l Sis."

"Take care, Big Bro."

"Luna says hi," he said to Theresa once they'd hung up. They sat there in silence for a while. Until Henning started retelling the island's history, then talking about an essayist he hoped to bring on board for the publisher. And finally Theresa told him about the new partner scheduled to join her accounting firm.

As midnight reached the island, they stood up, raised and clinked their glasses together, hugged, and wished each other Happy New Year. Arm in arm they gazed skyward and waited for a shooting star that never fell.

As they lay in bed, Henning would have liked to make love to Theresa. Thinking about the French guy aroused him. The French guy wasn't part of the family at table 24, neither of the kids were his, presumably he was a friend the family had invited along for the festivities. Even from a distance Henning saw how he stared straight at Theresa's breasts.

Theresa turned away, saying she was tired, and too drunk. Henning thought *it* might come, but then he fell asleep. Albeit not for long.

He lifts his head. Something's up. A car rushes past, far too close, almost grazing his bike, but he's too distracted to be afraid. The landscape is the same, the rockface is just a little closer than before. The roadside is bordered by black scree and fleshy, star-shaped plants. Suddenly he picks up a scent. Spicy, with a hint of sweetness. A little ways off lies another dream villa with lush bougainvillea pouring over its walls. Could their scent possibly reach him from there? He sniffs so deeply he gets dizzy. His lungs are too full. Too much CO_2 remains in his blood. Too much CO_2 triggers fear, which leads to even more frenzied breathing. Ever since *it* began haunting him, he's become all too familiar with the vicious cycle of hyperventilation. Just as he aims to bring his breath back under control, he's struck by a lightning bolt piercing his conscience with an image: his mother's bathroom.

It was filled with fist-sized stones, polished to a deep-black, round perfection. Evenings, his mother would paint them with all sorts of creatures—crabs, fish, seahorses, scorpions, all composed solely of colorful dots. They were gorgeous to look at, but for little Henning and Luna they were strictly taboo. Look but don't touch. Selling these stones at craft fairs, and later online, their mother earned a little on the side.

When she wasn't there, sometimes Henning and Luna would sneak into her bathroom to play with these forbidden treasures. They probably never managed to put everything back in the right order—four stones near the sink, two big ones in the shower, all the rest in the room's various corners—but their mother either never noticed or didn't care to notice. Her bathroom was her sanctuary. The walls were lined with pictures, including children's drawings, taped to the tiles. Next to the sink was an armchair where she'd sit and read, or just stare up at the ceiling when she couldn't do a thing anymore, which was often the case.

Henning never wondered where she got these smooth stones. Now it strikes him that, black as they were, they could easily have come from Lanzarote. But something else shakes him. The scent. Spicy and sweet. That's exactly how his mother's bathroom smelled. And he knows where that scent came from. It wasn't perfume or shower gel, it was a skin cream that came in a round, brown glass jar. Sometimes little Luna would twist the top off and sniff it when she really missed their mother. Henning can still picture the label, lined with a red border, which read: "La Belleza Atlántica." Back then the words bore an air of mystery, like the name of some pirate's island or a distant galaxy. The label also had a tiny drawing of a succulent with plump, star-shaped leaves. He also recalls the line of text at the bottom of the little label: "Hecho en Canarias."

Henning concentrates on breathing, exhale, exhale, exhale, inhale, tensing his abs and pushing the remaining air out of his lungs, and realizes it would be better to think about something else.

New year, new you.

The need to control your own thoughts is probably the worst aspect of *it*. But Henning still isn't sure whether "mental hygiene" even helps. When he tries to avoid unhelpful thoughts, it sends his mind spinning, his thoughts run off like hunted deer. Because *it* can call absolutely anything into action. His mother's bathroom, for instance. It stands for her despairing exhaustion, brought about by Henning and Luna, whose mere existence made them responsible for her suffering. Even though she was the person they loved most in the entire world. *It* opens its eyes.

Henning thinks about Bibbi and Jonas, their cute faces, but then it occurs to him that at any moment they could fall ill, or have an accident, and then everything would fall apart. *It* picks up the scent.

Henning thinks about his job, which he's so grateful to have. Which he loved doing, before the kids were born. But now he mostly sees it as a growing mountain of work that he keeps putting off, because even working overtime each night there's never enough time, he can't keep up. He always lags behind.

Too many emails in his inbox, too many manuscripts on his desk. Too many meetings with the publisher, which rob him of so much precious time. After vacation it'll be particularly bad. He'll never be able to catch up on a two-week backlog. *It* stretches its limbs.

Even thinking about everything he still needs or wants to do is dangerous: ride more, call his mother more often, read a novel again for once, finally clear out the storage space. *It* crouches down.

But then it occurs to him that, objectively speaking, he really doesn't have it so bad! Other people are worse off but still manage to balance it all better. Maybe Henning is doing something fundamentally wrong, maybe he's missing some skill other people have, and he doesn't even know what.

Sometimes he thinks something about his life is just off. Maybe behind this world there's another world, one where things have other meanings. Then he sees the kids and senses something evil within them, something devilish, demonic, a grinning, grotesque face lurking beneath their innocent expressions. Or maybe one day they'll just disappear without a trace, from one moment to the next, as if they'd never even existed. Theresa wouldn't remember a thing, and would think Henning was going mad as he desperately asked her where the kids were. *It* pounces.

New year, new you.

Henning shifts gears, pushes down harder on the pedals, and forces himself to keep breathing calmly.

The first time *it* showed up almost two years ago, he thought it was just an upset stomach or an infection of some sort. He remembers the exact day: February 2, 2016. Bibbi was three months old and screamed a lot, especially at night. Jonas had just decided he didn't want to go to nursery school anymore, and made a terrible scene each morning. At work Henning was butting heads with an author who hadn't finished his book, even though it had already been announced in their catalogue. Theresa was on parental leave and unhappy about it, since breastfeeding stressed her out.

When a bit of calm came in the afternoons

—Bibbi had finally fallen asleep, Theresa had taken Jonas for a swim—Henning would lie on the living room couch and savor every scream-free second without all the moaning and groaning, but at the same time he dreaded the possibility that they could disrupt him again at any moment. He had to relax, urgently, at least for a half hour or so, ideally get some shut-eye, because every fiber of his being cried out: I can't do it anymore.

But the more he tried to rest, the faster his heart beat. The pit of his stomach tingled, as if he were facing something anxiety-inducing, a public presentation, a tough talk with one of his authors, a flight. As his bowels began making noise, Henning thought he was getting sick. He thought: No wonder. And: That's just what I needed. Some shitty bug from that shitty nursery school. He had to run to the bathroom. He lurched to the toilet, full of self-loathing, because his immune system had failed, because he couldn't hold up under his burdens, because he just couldn't do enough to take care of Theresa and the kids. He imagined how a stomach flu would ravage him. How he'd have to lie in bed as Theresa did everything alone, growing ever more resentful. How Jonas and Bibbi would constantly whine and cry. And how he'd infect the whole family, and there'd be nobody left to clean up the puke, change the linens, and run to the pharmacy.

From the bathroom he returned to the couch. He'd have liked to make some tea, but he felt too weak. He laid down, and his ears started to ring. Tinnitus, he thought, this noise will never go away, and with that thought the first wave of cold fear swept through him. His arms started to itch, his skin hurt in certain spots, as if he'd stepped from intense cold back into the heat. His mouth was dry, his throat so tight he could barely swallow. He felt like he wasn't getting any air, and jumped up to open the window.

Then he started stumbling. His heart beat wildly, suddenly paused, leapt a few times, then returned to frenzied beating. Until it paused again.

Henning didn't know what was happening to him. He only knew it had to stop, straightaway, because he couldn't bear it. He ran circles around the living room, yanked at his hair, slapped himself in the head. At some point his heart began beating regularly again. He could breathe again. Bibbi started crying. Thankful for the distraction, he went to get the baby and carried her around the house saying "shhh-shhh," calming himself down.

Henning didn't tell Theresa about the episode. He sought out a cardiologist, who did an EKG and an ultrasound and found everything in perfect working order. Many people have erratic heartbeats every now and then, most don't even notice it. It can have a number of causes: one's disposition, stress, digestive problems. As long as the tests come out okay, there's no cause for alarm. Henning was to go home and enjoy life to the fullest. And maybe do something to reduce his stress.

Henning took this as the worst possible diagnosis. If he wasn't ill, then there was no cure, nothing he could treat.

Since then *it* has paid him a visit whenever it so chooses. It starts in his diaphragm, which burns like a combination of stage fright and fear of flying. His heart begins racing, then tripping up. Henning's body and mind go out of control. Sometimes it wakes him in the middle of the night. He startles from his sleep, can't get any air, has to go to the bathroom, and feels the urge to scream or bash his head against the wall but refrains so as not to wake anyone else. Instead he paces the hallway, the living room, the kitchen, until his heart steadies, *it* loosens its grip and grants Henning a half hour of relief, a lousy shred of luck, the pathetic joy of having once more survived.

Between these fits he's tormented by fears of the next fit. They make it difficult for him to even notice anything else. For Henning, life has become one long chain of interconnected internal states: bad, really bad, and half-good. Gorgeous weather and career success no longer affect him. That's all a mere backdrop. Sometimes he looks at Theresa and the kids and knows he loves them but doesn't feel a thing. For the most part, the kids magnify his fears. Their weakness, their dependence, their demands. The notion he could end up in the psych ward and no longer be able to be there for them. The worst part is that he can no longer think in peace the way he did before, for minutes or even hours on end, without danger looming on every side.

Oddly, none of this is even noticeable from the outside. Other people speak to him normally, look him in the eye, pose questions, and crack jokes that should make him laugh. But inside he's only focused on thinking the right thoughts to avoid waking *it* up, and on keeping his breathing under control. Despite it all, his fear of these episodes still allows him to function in everyday life. But they turn it into a living hell. He's all alone, trapped in his own personal purgatory.

As the months went by it became clear that *it* wouldn't just go away on its own. Henning tried everything. Letting *it* do its thing. Not fighting against *it*. Autogenic training. Progressive muscle relaxation. Cutting out alcohol, carbs, sugar. *It* stayed. Finally he told Theresa. She said it was burnout and recommended he see a psychologist.

Henning doesn't want to see a psychologist, even the mere thought of the cardiologist causes *it* to raise its head. Instead he pokes around online, reading about stress disorders, fatigue-related syndromes, exhaustion, and depression. Everything he reads about their causes seems to fit his circumstances. But they fit everyone else he knows, too: Theresa, his colleagues, Luna, his mother. He drills down into the most relevant websites: panic attacks, generalized anxiety disorder. Almost everything he's read, he's recognized, it precisely describes what he's enduring. It's just that there's absolutely no clear reason why these symptoms are happening to him, of all people. He repeatedly tells himself: Life is going fine! Better than for most people. He has no right nor reason to have a stress disorder. He has a good marriage, two healthy kids, a nice apartment complete with home office, no pressing financial precarity. They take at least one vacation a year. He even likes his job. Bibbi's gradually putting the worst behind her, Jonas has gotten used to having a little sister, both go to nursery school and don't get sick any more often than all the other kids. Maybe they're a little more demanding than average, but Theresa and

Henning firmly believe that's just a conse-
quence of above-average intelligence.

There's no convincing reason for *its* presence. *It* has nothing to do with Henning.
Other than the fact that it's living inside
him. Like a beast, a parasite, an alien about
to pop out of his belly. In days of yore people
might've called it a demon, maybe Henning
would have undergone an exorcism.

The bike ride is helping. It's like the fear is
draining from his stomach into his legs,
where it's quickly burnt off. His heartbeat is
regular. *It* has retreated, gone back to sleep.
He'd like to spend the rest of his life on this
bike. Fundamentally, he thinks, I'm totally
normal right now. A guy on vacation, on his
bike, battling only the wind, spurred onward
by the magnificent view. The primeval landscape. A New Year's ride through timeless
terrain, a world with no past.

As the next car drives by, Henning gets a
whiff of a cloying, cheap perfume. The one
after that spreads a scent of aftershave in its
wake. One smells of cigarette smoke, another
of sweaty men. Henning has never noticed
that you can smell the passengers in passing

cars. It's like the star-shaped plants have opened something within him, a channel between nose and brain, through which the fulsome world now flows.

Henning smells a herd of spotted goats before he sees it. They leisurely stroll through the scree under the watch of sheepdogs, nibbling here and there at stalks you'd never think were edible. Some of the goats are pregnant and look almost wider than they are long. Their enormous bellies push outward, swaying to and fro like a bloated piece of baggage.

Just as Henning is about to turn his attention elsewhere, he spots the herdsman. His dark garb almost blends in with the backdrop. He's a good ways away from the road, standing amid the herd, looming over the animals like a signpost in the empty landscape. He's wearing a dark cap and a cloth covers his face, leaving only his eyes visible. Protection from the dust and wind, thinks Henning, that makes sense. But it still seems strange. The man looks straight at him. From this distance Henning can't actually see his eyes, but the guy's facing in his direction and standing utterly still, not moving even as the herd he's supposed to be watching slowly moves onward. As Henning rides away, slogging against the wind and the ascent, the herdsman's gaze follows him. He seems to turn without moving his legs, like a puppet in a haunted house train ride. There's something else that's strange. The herd doesn't make even the slightest sound— no goats bleating, no dogs barking. It must be because he's upwind. As Henning glances back a half kilometer or so later, the herds-man is still standing there, without his goats, who've followed the dogs and moved quite a way along.

Henning has to think back to last night. The dinner at Las Olas began wrapping up around twenty to nine. The plates were cleared, the glasses hadn't been refilled for a while already. Soon the guests of this first shift would be invited to head home, so preparations could be made for the second shift. The music was turned up again as everyone left. Henning recognized one of his secret favorites, "Ai Se Eu Te Pego," a hit from summers past. He found it a bit pitiful how much he liked the song. There was something so catchy about it, the beat went straight to his bones. After he'd heard it for the first time, he'd gone straight to YouTube and watched the video. The singer was onstage at a club, and looked like a jovial kid. The kind of young guy who listens to the radio, singing and dancing along, copying pop stars' moves. "Ai se eu te pego," "Ooh, if I get my hands on you." It had to be about sex. A man-child standing onstage in joyful innocence, performing a song about sex for a crowd of women who idolized him.

It was this crowd that led Henning to watch the video over and over. It really did consist almost exclusively of women. But not just any women. A veritable collection of beauty queens danced at the foot of the stage, blondes and brunettes, thin and curvaceous, sweet and sassy, dashing and elegant. Not only were these women gorgeous, they also seemed approachable and pleasant, every single one was like the girl next door, but with the face and figure of a princess. Henning couldn't get enough, they were so cheerful, they were enjoying the show so much, they were dancing so innocently and blowing kisses at the singer. Ooh, if I get my hands on you.

And what an unbelievable coincidence, to think that anywhere in the whole wide world so many beautiful women happened to gather in the same club, probably in Lisbon.

This earworm had been stuck in Henning's head for days, and he kept watching the video, even at work. Until it occurred to him: of course that crowd was the result of a casting call. Maybe not the entire crowd, but definitely the first few rows. Those weren't mere concertgoers, they were models. Prototypes. Maybe they'd come from all over Europe. Henning couldn't believe it had taken him days to realize that. And he found the realization as calming as it was disappointing.

So he automatically started smiling as the first few notes rang out at Las Olas. *Sábado na balada*. The kids popped up out of nowhere and began pulling at his hands. They wanted to hit the dance floor, which was little more than a slightly larger space between the tables. A few tourists were already there, clapping, stamping their feet, moving to the beat.

Henning didn't want to make a fool of himself, but he was happy the kids had come to him. Normally they run to Theresa whenever they want something. When they're injured or sick or tired or hungry. Even when they want to be held, or are looking for something, or are playing a game and get stuck. And Theresa says: "You have a father, and he has hands and feet, so why don't you ask him?" And casts annoyed glances in his direction, as if it were his fault the kids preferred her.

Years ago Henning had edited a book about childrearing, and it sold so well that to this day it pays his salary. The title was *The Constructed Self*, and it made the case that children were pushed by their environments—meaning their parents—into certain roles. And they continued playing those parts, sticking to them, for their entire lives.

When Henning worked with the author on this book, he himself hadn't had kids yet. Nor had the author, which somehow hadn't struck Henning or his publisher as cause for doubt; the author had, after all, studied neurophysiology and the social sciences. And anyway, the sales proved them right in all regards.

Now Henning knows the book is utter nonsense. Kids are what they are. Since early childhood Jonas has gravitated toward backhoes and Bibbi toward dolls, even though neither Henning nor Theresa conform to classic gender roles. And they cry out for Mama, not Papa. Bibbi and Jonas aren't interested in the modern-day rules of emancipation. They want Mama because she's Mama. Henning's destiny lies in becoming the victim of books like *The Constructed Self*. If parents' behavior determines children's character, then it's Henning's fault that the kids annoy Theresa with their neediness. That's why Theresa is so irritable, and sometimes spends days on end on the verge of exploding. Because she views their children's dependence on her, their mother, as the result of Henning's inability to fulfill his role as their father.

But he's ready to. He wants to. He believes.

It's not his fault the kids don't want him.

But then last night they dragged *him* to the dance floor, and he gladly went along. He bent over a bit to hold them by the hand, and let their rhythmless movements pull him this way and that. Other kids did the same with their parents. Henning even sang along, *Ai se eu te pego, ai se eu te pego,* and Bibbi's eyes grew wide as the foreign words flowed from his lips. He lifted her up and whirled her in a circle and then Jonas. It was so fun they whooped with joy.

Until Henning spotted the cute couple dancing. It took a few seconds for him to recognize Theresa. At first it was just some couple, man and woman, their bodies entwined, two pieces of the same puzzle. A two-headed being with four legs, his left side embracing her right side, their arms held as if they were about to tango.

The small crowd on the dance floor parted, making way for the couple. Their steps were completely in sync, as if they'd spent years practicing for this moment. Clearly "Ai Se Eu Te Pego" was the perfect dance music. Some guests stood up, watched, and clapped.

People made space for the dancers. The Frenchman held Theresa tight, as if he'd never let her go. Then he suddenly pushed her outward, holding her hand as she did a twirl under his arm, and pulled her back in. She tossed her head back and laughed so loud it was audible over the music.

Henning and the kids also stopped, stood, and stared. Jonas asked: "Who's that guy?" Bibbi looked like she was about to cry. Her horrified face made it clear to Henning exactly what was happening. He felt nothing, no envy, no anger, as if something in him had died. Something blew cold deep within. Then the gulf closed back up. Henning and the kids went back to table 27 before the song was over. Henning started clearing their places and packing everything up. He said goodnight to Katrin and Karlchen.

"That was fun," he said.

Theresa returned to the table and linked arms with him, slightly sweaty.

"He sure can dance," she said, waving goodbye to Katrin and Karlchen as they headed toward the exit.

New year, new you.

The next time Henning looks up, the cliff is a whole lot closer. Too much, going by the hour and his speed. As if some invisible giant had shoved the mountain closer while he wasn't looking, just to play a joke on him. Maybe it's an optical trick of the angled sunlight. He is now at the mouth of the canyon. A few more kilometers and he'll be at the rock face. Henning grows fearful. Not a neurotic fear, a real fear. He's scared of the mountain. Scared as if something dangerous were looming over him, and he didn't know if he'd be able to conquer it.

Already the road is fairly steep. On either side of the road the star-shaped plants are growing scarce, and the scree descends to a rugged canyon floor. Henning pushes the gearshift. He planned to save the lowest gears for the very end, so he'd still have a reserve for when the ascent became too taxing. But now he has to downshift if he doesn't want to fall over. He shifts the front gears, eighth, seventh, sixth, fifth, only in fourth gear can he really pedal onward. His tempo has slowed to match his pedaling pace. He rises up from the saddle.

It's not a matter of speed. It's a matter of just doing it. His legs need a break, but Henning wants to save his breaks for when the really steep ascent begins. If only this wind would let up. Without the wind it'd be no problem. His mouth is dry, his throat raw, every breath hurts. The fact that he brought no water is a bad joke. His shoes, too, are a joke, his toes feel like they've been pounded with a hammer. He can barely even feel the sore spots between his thighs anymore.

I have to keep my nerve, he thinks. Not fight, not get angry, just keep my eyes on the next two feet. Press onward stoically, sensing, knowing it's possible. That every foot can be covered, and every next foot. Because if he manages to cover one foot at a time, he'll manage the whole mountain.

Inhale-exhale-exhale. Inhale-exhale-exhale.

Henning increases his breath rate, one pedal stroke in, two strokes out, and pays extra attention to fully emptying his lungs. At this faster pace he has to push his breath out, and it whistles through his teeth.

Think about something else. Not the mountain.

After he and Theresa had drunk their wine out on the patio and toasted to the New Year, they went to the bathroom to get ready for bed. Why should they stay up any later, if the kids would be up and raring to go by six? While brushing her teeth, Theresa started talking about the Frenchman. Henning didn't know why. Maybe she was trying to torture him. Or maybe she was just happy to enjoy a good flirt, since Henning clearly meant nothing to her. She was talking to him like a close acquaintance. He was just a listener, she could just dump all her experiences into his ready ears.

The entire time she'd stood near table 24 chatting, the Frenchman had stared at her. He'd sat like a stranger at the table, not talking to anyone else, looking only at Theresa, as if she were the only other human being in the entire room. At some point he'd told her that her eyes were like stars, and she'd shot back that they were more like x-ray machines. They'd both laughed so hard they'd teared up. That broke the ice. They'd had a great conversation. In French, of course. Not that Theresa's French was so good. She just lacked inhibitions. In her view, communication is a matter of will, at least within Europe. You just have to want it. She uses as many foreign words as she can, pins some suffixes on, pronounces everything the way she thinks people there would say it, and voilà. It works. Even the Spaniards on Lanzarote understand her. Henning is afraid of communication failure. He feels silly and helpless abroad, and is thrilled when he needn't even speak in English. Theresa just dives right in, blathering at anyone and everyone, and then reproaches Henning for letting her do everything on her own.

And from that moment on it was clear what the Frenchman wanted from Theresa. No, he didn't want to screw, he wanted to dance. Theresa enjoyed playing coy while he pursued her all night through glances, gestures, words. When she came over to the table to check on the kids, he drew her right back into conversation.

"He downright stalked me," Theresa said with a laugh.

"And in the end he won," said Henning.

"It was great." Theresa spit her toothpaste

into the sink. "Great song. We were a perfect match. I'd never experienced anything like it."

"Why are you telling me all this?" asked Henning.

"Because you're my husband," she replied. "Because I don't want to hide anything from you."

Henning had no idea what it was she didn't want to hide from him. He only knew *it* gave a stir. In bed he placed his hand on her hip, but then she turned away.

Tired. Too drunk.

The wind picks up. It's still a more formidable opponent than gravity. Each time Henning thinks it can't possibly blow any harder, a gust pushes him to a near standstill and he nearly falls over. Now he won't look past his front wheel and the asphalt. He concentrates on his musculoskeletal system. He keeps checking in with his body, conjuring up each individual muscle and telling it to relax, not to cramp up. He senses which muscle groups are essential to his progress, and which he can let rest. He pushes the pedal harder with his left leg for three strokes, then with his right, to give each side a bit of a break. The wind almost seems embodied as it counters him. As if it were a living being that would do almost anything to keep him from reaching the peak.

That night was atrocious. Over the last two years he's had a lot of awful nights, but last night set a new record on the scale of horrors. *It* woke him at two. Maybe it felt worse precisely because Henning had just started feeling a little more secure. Because he'd been dumb enough to believe that here on Lanzarote nothing could happen to him.

Time and time again he'd read online that you can't die of a panic attack, no matter how it might feel, no matter how fierce it is. It's a physical state of emergency with no lasting negative effects. But telling yourself that doesn't help. Henning was convinced he wouldn't survive the night. His heart went into such a frenzy it had nothing to do with mere arrhythmia. It felt more like an epileptic seizure. Henning ran in circles in the yard, below a majestic, broad, starry sky laced by the shooting stars he and Theresa had waited for in vain. He silently cried out to the universe, begging for help. Asking that it rip open his chest and tear out whatever it was that was tormenting him. He wanted to call a doctor, but knew that when they finally got him to the hospital they'd find nothing. When his heart began beating normally again, he collapsed onto the black gravel and cried in relief.

Shortly after he'd gone back to bed and, contrary to all expectations, fallen back asleep around five, Theresa's phone rang, waking him again. It was her parents. They just wanted to wish her Happy New Year and hadn't thought about the time difference. Lying on his back, eyes closed, he listened to Theresa's grumbled replies. He also overheard what her parents were saying. Rolf and Marlies always shout into the phone as if they believed their voices had to cover the distance through their own sheer force. They often sit together in front of the phone, loudspeaker turned up, with all the enthusiasm of latecomers who've managed to decode this one smartphone secret. They even share an e-mail address, RoMa4852@web.de, and are proud of the fact that their first names' initial syllables combine to spell the name of the city they've lived in for a few years now.

"The constant wind," Theresa grumbles into the phone. "You can hardly take the kids outside. The little town house is nice, but too small, really. And the landscape, sure, it's impressive enough, but it also takes some getting used to."

On the phone with her parents, Theresa puts her unflappable optimism on pause. She quits trying to "make the best" of everything. Instead, she complains about even the smallest trifle.

When Henning's on the phone with his mother, he always restricts himself to telling her how great everything is going. At work, at home with the family, with Theresa, and especially on vacation. He reports on how everything is "functioning" to perfection. For the rest of his life, he never ever wants to be a burden on his mother, not even on the phone.

Rolf and Marlies asked if Theresa had enjoyed her New Year's, and told her about the parties on the streets of Rome, especially the one in Piazza Trilussa, near where they live. She bitterly replied that it was hard to really let loose with two kids in tow. Henning opened his eyes and caught her haggard gaze. He was glad Rolf and Marlies had called. Lying here while Theresa was on the phone felt so marvelously normal. And they always agreed that Rolf and Marlies were annoying.

As usual, Theresa's parents launched into their duet: they felt sorry for her, and gave advice on how she might improve the situation. If it's too windy, you could go to a nice museum. Maybe she could hire a babysitter, so they could have a night out to celebrate. And maybe they could rent one of the neighboring town houses, so they wouldn't feel so cramped. The more absurd their recommendations, the angrier Theresa grew. After ten minutes she said "Okay, bye," and hung up.

They stayed in bed for a bit and griped about her parents. How self-centered they were, how unworldly, how tactless. It felt good to complain about Rolf and Marlies together. Like any other morning, as if nothing unusual had happened during the night. At some point Jonas came into their bedroom, and Bibbi began crying in her crib. As Henning went to get up, his knees gave out. He had to sit on the edge of the bed for a few more minutes.

"What's up?" asked Theresa.

"Just a bit dizzy," he answered.

The bike doesn't have drop bars. So he needs extra strength from his back and arms. In order to minimize drag, he leans his upper body onto the handlebars, bracing his elbows on the grips and his hands on the stem. It's uncomfortable, but it works. Different muscle groups now pitch in, and drag decreases. Henning's face is now looking directly at the asphalt. He sees how porous the road's top layer is. The wind carries little pebbles up the steep slope. A dust devil spins. An ant makes its way toward the other side. A lizard lying right in the way of his front wheel darts to the side. Its greenish back glistens, and it looks like a miniature version of those monstrous marine iguanas from the Galápagos. It stops just two feet away, as if certain someone like Henning wouldn't do it any harm.

To stay oriented, Henning follows the

direction of the road's edge. He's happy that, hunched over like this, he can no longer see the looming massif. As long as he can't see it, the present moment is all that counts. The fact that, no matter how slowly, he's still making progress. He finds a new rhythm, inhale, exhale-exhale, inhale, exhale-exhale. Fourth gear functions ideally, his tempo stays steady. Even his thoughts start to flow. Rolf and Marlies. A good topic. You can think about them a whole lot without ever finding yourself on thin ice.

Once or twice a year they come to Göttingen to babysit their grandkids, as they put it. They get a ride from the airport in Hannover and end up standing around in Henning and Theresa's kitchen, too excited to sit down. They talk about the gifts they've brought, without having asked in advance what the kids actually like. A model car and a stuffed animal from an oh-so-charming artisanal shop in Rome. They're so taken with themselves that they fail to notice the kids don't even like this stuff. Only when coffee and cake appear on the table are they ready to take a seat. As they eat, they yammer on and on, mostly with one another, as if they hadn't seen each other in ages. Rolf tells Marlies how lucky they were to find that apartment in Rome. Marlies asks Rolf if he, like she, finds German artisans far superior to Roman ones. They tease one another, correct one another, and enlist Henning and Theresa as audience for a conversation they clearly find riveting and hilarious, all the while thoroughly ignoring Bibbi and Jonas until they start whining and bickering. Then Rolf and Marlies shoot each other a glance, with a we'd-better-not-say-anything-now expression on their faces, a raised eyebrow, a slight shake of the head, a huff hovering over the plate. When it comes to raising and disciplining children it's best to stay out of it. Even if Theresa and Henning really are doing it all wrong.

At some point Henning leaves the room, taking the kids to play Legos and leaving Theresa to chat with her parents in the kitchen. Over the following days they set up a grandma-grandpa-grandkids schedule for Rolf and Marlies: playground, park, zoo. They pack some snacks, and give a few tips about how to organize everything so Bibbi can still have her nap. They calm Jonas down, soothing his frustration as he seeks to get his grandparents' attention, to no avail. If even once Rolf turns toward the kids—crouching down beside Jonas in front of an animal enclosure at the zoo, for instance, sticking his arm out to point at something, and reciting a couple of clever yet inappropriate factoids about the Persian fallow deer —Marlies digs her phone out of her purse to get a snapshot of his well-practiced happy-grandpa face.

Henning knows she prints these pictures, frames them, and displays them on the dresser in their apartment in Rome. He knows they look at these pictures and are thrilled by the wonderful relationship they have with their grandkids. The very idea stokes his aggression.

As they're driven back to the airport a few days later, they chat about what a marvelous family weekend they all had together. How glad they are to support Theresa and Henning by helping out. And of course they just can't resist sharing a couple of child-rearing tips at the very end. The kids are given far, far too much attention. You don't need to give everything so much weight. Regular mealtimes, clear boundaries. Beyond that, they'll simply grow up on their own.

What bothers Henning the most is his suspicion that Rolf and Marlies just might be right. When Theresa was little they handed her off to relatives so they could go on vacation alone. They certainly never crawled around the house on all fours looking for a lost pacifier or whatever stuffed animal happened to be her favorite that day. Above all, they'd never have even thought about playing with their daughter. Kids play with kids, adults converse with adults. And Theresa grew up into a perfectly normal adult. She's healthy, has a solid grip on herself and her life, and doesn't have any emotional scars. If Rolf and Marlies's approach was a success, Henning can't help but wonder why he and Theresa go to such great lengths to treat their kids with such love and respect. But he already knows the answer to that, at least for himself: because that's just how it's done. His approach to Bibbi and Jonas doesn't follow any conceptual theory. He treats them the only way he knows how.

Nevertheless Rolf and Marlies did manage to create a family of sorts for Theresa—compared to what Henning's childhood household was like, at any rate. Not that it took much. Henning's father Werner practically never even knew him. Sometimes he'd call, when he was drunk. He'd want to talk to the kids, and would blabber a bunch of sappy nonsense at them. That he loved them, and would come pick them up one day. It scared Luna and Henning. Even now, every few years Werner will send a birthday card, albeit invariably on the wrong date.

Their mother did everything she could to give Henning and Luna a tolerable home life. Their apartment's largest room, which would have been the living room, belonged to the kids, and was divided with a big curtain so they each had their own domain. Whenever there was some money left over, their mother bought them books, toys, or clothes. In all the years she was raising Henning and Luna, she never had any men over. As long as you're living with me, I belong to you two, she'd say.

And she was a beautiful woman, slim, with long blonde hair, always dressed in colorful blouses and jeans.

But she wasn't exactly radiant. Because of her back pain, she was often slightly hunched over. Her hair was dull and hung down lifelessly. Sometimes she couldn't even manage to put on makeup. She was always overtired, overworked, stressed out, irritated. Everything she did was accompanied by a string of complaints. She'd set the food on the table and say how long she'd slaved away at the stove. She'd do the laundry and lament how she had to spend her evening off washing and ironing. Henning and Luna lived with their heads held low. Their mother tidied up the apartment they'd made such a mess of, took care of problems at school they'd brought about, and took them to the doctor when they got sick. Because of them, she'd renounced friends, men, parties, travel, art, reading, films, theater, stimulating conversations, and a better job. Every day she declared how, because of them, she was condemned to a life that neither suited her nor pleased her. So they should at least take care not to make any extra work for her. As the older child, Henning should lighten her load by tending to chores around the house, and Luna should be a good little girl. She was on the brink of exhaustion, and couldn't do everything all by herself; after all, she was a human being, not a machine.

After such tirades she'd draw Henning and Luna into her arms and say: "But of course you're the most precious of all to me! You know that, right? You two are my number one prize!"

That was the worst. Henning detected her guilty conscience in the phrase "number one prize." She said the kids were her "number one prize" because she was ashamed that, secretly, she wished they'd just go to hell. Ever since he was little, he'd been used to viewing everything he did, said, or even thought as an assault on his mother's happiness. He wished often enough that he weren't alive. By fifteen he'd contemplated suicide, or at least moving out so as to unburden his mother of his presence. But there was Luna. She was too young, she needed him, and leaving her was utterly unthinkable. He waited until she turned sixteen to leave. He couldn't hold on any longer. He was nineteen and had completed his university entrance exams. When he moved out, she dropped out. Nothing in the world could convince her to stay home with their mother and finish high school. First she followed him to Leipzig, where he was a student, then to Göttingen, where he'd gotten his first job. And when he met Theresa, Luna started drifting from place to place.

Their mother was in her mid-forties when Henning and Luna moved out. She left her job and apartment and moved to Berlin. She still lives there, and works at a small gallery, paints, lounges in cafés, and tells him about concerts and openings during their phone calls. Henning is thrilled for her freedom, she deserves it more than anyone in the world. He hopes she has a boyfriend. When he asks, she laughs and says it's none of his business.

She isn't very interested in Bibbi and Jonas. She says she's cleaned enough baby's behinds for one lifetime. In comparison, Rolf and Marlies are really good grandparents. Henning and Theresa concur on that point after they've taken off again. But for days afterward they still feel ripe for the loony bin.

Henning has reached the start of the steepest part. Sometimes such inclines look steeper from afar than they do up close. A cliff can appear almost vertical but then grow optically gentler as you approach. Clearly this isn't the case with the massif leading up to Femés. The road climbs before him like a ramp, and the first few pedal strokes make it clear he'll have to downshift straightaway. He vows to stay in third gear until at least the first switchback, then shift to second, and save first for the final segment. After just a few feet he realizes it's a vow he can't keep. He has to go right to first gear. And now the incline proves it can indeed be a more formidable opponent than the wind. His bike has become a stair-climber with steps too high and a tempo too slow to maintain the pace. Henning would actually be faster if he dismounted and just pushed. But that's out of the question. He'll allow himself to take breaks—as few as possible, as many as strictly necessary—and will conquer this mountain on his bike. He tries standing up off the saddle, but the shape of the bike isn't suited for it. He breaks into enough of a sweat that the wind no longer dries it. Within seconds he feels his back grow damp; he's wearing a T-shirt made of cotton, hardly as functional as synthetic sportswear. His quads begin to throb. His throat feels like sandpaper, and he feels a tugging at his temples that might come from dehydration. Henning starts silently chanting, in sync with each push:

Damn-wind, damn-wind, damn-wind.

The chant summons rage. At the wind—why does it have to be so strong, today of all days, and from all directions? At the mountain—how the hell can anything be so steep? At the cars, which are passing too close. At the bike, which doesn't have any lower gears.

Damn-wind.

The rage bestows strength. He doesn't have to push as hard. It's an all-encompassing rage. Not just at the road, the wind, and the mountain. It's a rage directed at everything, a furious energy field, like heat or light. Henning is burning inside.

Damn-job, damn-*it*, damn-world.

Henning clutches the handlebars, his knuckles turn white. He gives his all with each stroke, like his muscles were on the verge of tearing apart.

Damn-Theresa, damn-Theresa, damn-Theresa.

That doesn't really fit the beat, but nevertheless feels good.

Damn-Jonas, damn-kids, damn-family.

Henning is at war. He draws on all his reserves. And something rises within him. Something he can use. Then, something that's too much. It wants up, it wants out. Henning wants to hold it back, push it down, but by then it's happened. His head chants:

Damn-Bibbi, damn-Bibbi, damn-Bibbi.

He can't stop it. It keeps going.

Damn-Bibbi, damn-Bibbi.

The rage has found its flashpoint, its center, the volcanic core from which this lava bursts forth. Henning is crying. He's bawling with abandon, and can no longer see through the tears.

Damn-Bibbi.

He's no longer thinking it, he's screaming. He has zero idea what he means by it. There isn't a soul in the world he loves more. But the rage wields tremendous power.

Damn-Bibbi!

Looking around, he discovers he's halfway up. It comes as a shock. He can't believe he's this high already. He sticks to it, standing up to press against the wind. The tears have dried, the rage has gone silent. He stretches his back, looks down into the valley. The road he's traveled looks tiny, like the route of a model train set, just a narrow little ribbon that in this very moment is entirely empty, as if the source endlessly churning cars out into the world had suddenly run dry.

Henning smiles. Despite his exhaustion he feels strong. He looks upward, the pass looks near. Not a soul is in sight atop the overlook, the restaurants must still be closed. He pulls his phone out of the patch pocket on his cycling shorts. Ten o'clock in the morning on New Year's Day. He can't believe he's only been riding for two hours. Now he's sure he'll make it. But he still warns himself to be humble. He's only just cleared the first half of the rock face, the second will be longer and harder, no matter what mathematicians might say. It's the exact opposite of a vacation, whose second half always goes by twice as fast.

As he sets the bike back on track, uses the tip of his toes to put the right pedal at the right height, and puts all his weight on it to get moving again, he nearly keels over. At the last moment he manages to stop the bike from striking the asphalt. The wind and gradient prevent him from getting enough momentum to stay balanced. He sets the bike perpendicular to the roadway, puts his right foot back on the pedal, shoves off with his left, and rides off. At an angle, despite the slope, getting started is no problem. Henning reaches the other side of the road, curves back, stays diagonal to the slope. Speeding up just a tad over the last few feet, he swings into the next part. This way he's basically dividing the ascent into tiny portions, making switchbacks within switchbacks, battling through each turn, and then momentarily relaxing along each diagonal. He won't cover the distance as quickly, but he'll be moving forward. Slow and steady as a snail. He rides on.

The way he burst into tears now strikes him as strange, the sudden rage at Bibbi seems senseless and unfair. He's ashamed of it. Maybe it's the lack of water, which is making him dazed and confused. Or just exhaustion.

Before falling asleep last night, he had a vision, like the start of a dream, but he was still fully conscious. He saw the Frenchman, and how he threw himself at Theresa. Everything was crystal clear. Theresa lay on a couch with bright, oriental-patterned upholstery. The room was more like a grand hall, with a square plan, and high as a tower. There was a glass dome in the middle of the ceiling, through which bright rays of sun cascaded. Plants grew rampant from pots suspended by long chains. Henning saw the bare walls, the tile floor, and felt the cool air of this space. Above the couch a wooden double door led to the outside. Half of the door was open, so Henning could see out. No doubt, this house was on Lanzarote. He saw the balustrade of a large terrace, and behind it palm trees, cacti, pepper trees, and a volcanic panorama. It must have been one of the houses he'd gawked at for so long, first on-line, then in real life. Whitewashed walls, vast garden.

The Frenchman was lying on top of Theresa, his pants were down, and his upper body was bare. And Henning recognized every detail of him, too. He saw dark, wind-blown hair, the triangular masculine torso, the curved shoulder blades, the taut buttocks. Dark hair grew on either side of his spine, like a road divided into two lanes.

Of course Henning had never seen the Frenchman naked in real life. Nor did he know the house. Despite that, the image was detailed and clear as day. But there was no movement, it was like a film still. This vision ought to have been disturbing, but Henning felt nothing. He tried to think of something else, the image faded, he fell asleep.

Shortly after that he dreamt that Bibbi had fallen into water. He didn't see how she'd fallen, she'd just gone under, her light body in dark water, sinking. He had to dive in after her, save her, right away. But he was afraid his dive might disturb the muck below, muddying the water so he wouldn't be able to see anything. Then he'd fruitlessly grope around, twisting and turning, desperately grabbing after Bibbi with his hands, half-blind beneath the surface, without finding her. This thought was so terrifying that he did nothing. He stood there pondering. Should he try to carefully slide into the water? But how would that work? He knew he had to act fast, the outline of Bibbi was already just a blur, she was sinking deeper, she was almost out of sight, he had to do it, but fear paralyzed him, he could already imagine how it would feel to reach his arms out for her only to find nothing, but still that was his only option, he had to go in and get her, now. Instead of diving in, he woke up.

He lay on his back. *It* rattled him so hard that he instinctively reached out for Theresa. His fingers dug into her nightshirt and pulled. She woke with a scream. He hadn't wanted to do that.

Normally he'd never wake her, no matter how bad things were for him. With kids, sleep is too precious to be interrupted. And it's not like Theresa can do anything to help, anyway. After he'd told her about *it*, she had tried to be there for him. There was a phase in which she had tried to encourage him, held his hand, asked if he'd like a tisane, a hot water bottle, some music. They had tried having her read to him, watching TV, having sex. Nothing worked. On the contrary, the attacks got worse once Henning realized that not even Theresa could help. That *it* was stronger than she was.

Since then, Henning has tried to hide his attacks. He traipses through the house and tries not to wake anyone. And since they've started coming by day, too, he's even learned to act normal. His heart races and skips, he sweats, every muscle in his body tenses up. And he behaves as if it were nothing. He goes on talking, eating, playing with the kids, making phone calls. Sometimes he walks to the bathroom and looks in the mirror. He finds it unfathomable that *it* can't be seen. As his heart leaps into a crazy dance with potentially lethal pauses, his face looks like it always does. Maybe his eyes are a little red. Of course Theresa notices something is up, but she says nothing. *It* has become Henning's own private matter.

He'd woken her up that night by accident, in a panic, out of mere reflex. And this time she didn't try to help. Instead, she flipped out. As she screamed at him, she turned away, as if he were a stranger who'd slipped into her bed.

"I've had it up to here with your drama. What, you think everything revolves around you?"

With all his might, Henning tried to clench his jaw shut to stop his shivering. It seemed that something he had long expected was happening. Something awful. A complete and utter loss of all dignity.

"Your neuroses are hurting the whole family. Pull yourself together already!"

Henning's innards metamorphosed into a cold clump. For a few seconds he couldn't feel his own heartbeat. He was on the verge of losing consciousness. He wondered whether he and Theresa would ever recover from this.

"Be a man! A man I can love!"

Just as he thought nothing worse could happen, Theresa turned right around and fell back to sleep. She even started snoring a bit, as if to mock him. Henning escaped to the yard, where he ran in panicked circles.

In the morning, after her parents had called, Theresa stayed in bed while he got up and prepared breakfast. Because he wasn't hungry in the least, he took only three plates out of the cupboard. The table gave the impression Henning didn't exist anymore. Breakfast for a mother and her two kids.

He gets off his bike. His muscle metabolism is forcing him to take another break. He can't force his body to push one more pedal stroke. His left thigh is cramping up. He massages it with both hands, trying to relax the muscles. He'd best quit. He could push his bike up this last bit. But the pass isn't far off, maybe just 300 level feet higher, divided by another switchback. The last curve is razor-sharp. The very final stretch after this hairpin turn is precipitous. Henning has noticed how cars' engines rev up right here, as if the drivers struggled to even downshift into first. He's heard the engines roar.

From here the valley below is mere abstraction. Playa Blanca is a patch of white, worn along the edges, spread like a doormat before the glittering surface of the sea. The luxury homes are white dots on the dark landscape. A falcon darts past as Henning glances downslope. The only things that look the same are the volcanic mountains, whose silent panorama remains unchanged.

To stabilize his bike in the wind, Henning has parked the front wheel diagonally against one of the large stones providing notional protection between the road and the abyss. The gusts whistle and howl through the bike's frame, and through his helmet's air slits. Up here the wind is even less restrained, like an invisible waterfall rushing over the ridge. The valley seems oddly deserted. Was a weather advisory issued? Henning resists the impulse to check the forecast on his phone. It's a totally normal day on the Atlantic. The first day of the first month of 2018. If there's one thing that can be considered normal on an island, it's strong wind.

He spots something moving on the empty road. A car emerges from a fold in the land-scape below Henning, slowly at first, then faster. It enters the next curve, then disappears from view again. An old SUV, Toyota or Range Rover, there are a few on the island. Henning decides to wait until the car has passed; his zig-zag tactic requires the entire roadway. His tongue sticks to his gums, the pulling sensation under his temples has progressed to a dull throb. Alternating arms, he scratches his pits, where the skin is dry and itches like mad. He urgently needs water. His vision flickers, the sun is dazzling, and then there's the wind. Thinking ahead to the final stretch, he feels no resistance to the idea. His body is prepared to further obey his will. It frees up his last reserves of energy, carries oxygen to every last capillary. Ready to push past all its old limits.

Henning doesn't want to hurt the whole family with his neuroses. He wants to be a man worthy of being loved. He wants to laugh more, joke around more, see the funnier side of life's little everyday catastrophes. He wants to embrace Theresa more often, be less annoyed by the kids, just up and get together with friends more often. It can't be that hard. It can't be any harder than scaling a twenty-percent grade into a strong head-wind on a rental bike, at least.

The SUV is approaching. It's a Range Rover, in rusty dark blue. A woman is at the wheel. Henning can't see her face; as she drives by, she turns her head the other way, toward the mountain, as if she didn't want to be recognized. Her blonde hair is in a French braid, a style that has fallen out of fashion in recent years. Henning's mother used to wear her hair like that a lot. The Range Rover rounds the last turn, the motor howls, and it disappears between the restaurants.

Henning puts all his strength into pedaling. It goes surprisingly easily, he sits right back down onto the saddle, and his zig-zag approach helps him gain enough speed that the first few mini-switchbacks are no problem. His body freed up a shocking surplus of energy during his short break, and is now ready to go. Henning lowers his upper body and braces his arms on the handlebars. If he sits up, the wind will push him off the bike. Every now and then he lifts his gaze to estimate the remaining distance. It's shrinking, pedal stroke by pedal stroke. Henning decides not to take any more breaks, and to conquer this last stretch as one grand endgame. But right then his strength dissipates again, shockingly fast. He doesn't wear down slowly; instead, his entire energy supply abruptly cuts off.

He halts for just a minute, and waits for his muscles to come back to life. Then he rides onward.

The rock into which this road is carved is jagged and porous, in some areas rising into waves that look almost liquid. An entire planet churning itself out, petrified midflow, cooled into a solid as it was being created.

He has to pause again for a moment. And then he heads into the last curve. It, too, was no illusion: the road gets even steeper just before reaching the ridge. Now Henning lifts his gaze as he rides, keeping his eyes on the prize. The higher he climbs, the more of Femés he can see. He looks at the restaurant's panoramic window and, inside, chairs set upside down atop the tables. He sees the somnolent houses on this New Year's morning. Not a soul in sight. And then someone comes into view, a man in a hat, a Spaniard, clad in the traditional black garb of the islanders. He's standing in the yard of one of the houses at the edge of town, hose in hand, watering the plants. A gardener at work.

Henning looks away, concentrating again on his objective, the spot at the summit of the pass where the road disappears between the two restaurants. But something isn't right. It has to do with the gardener, there's something perplexing about him. Henning looks at him, then away again, then back at him, but can't figure out what he finds so bothersome. The man is standing with his back to Henning, his hat tilted far back. Henning feels a shiver, as if it's not really a human being. When he imagines the figure turning around, fear floods his body. Henning forces his attention back toward the road, just a few feet left between him and the crest, he can do it, he knew he'd be able to do it. Now he just has to not mess it up, carefully ride up to his goal, concentrate with all his might on each turn, and keep breathing, even if it hurts.

And that's when he realizes what's off. The

gardener is standing backwards. His back is to Henning, so he's facing into the wind. The water from the hose should be blown back, drenching him. The way he's standing should mean he can't water the plants. What this gardener is doing is completely impossible.

Henning reaches the highest point.

HE LEANS HIS bike against the wall and falls onto a built-in bench overlooking the small plaza in front of the church. The stone cools his thighs and back. For a moment, his aches dissipate. Henning's body collapses in on itself, his mind goes quiet. He feels the sun's heat and the wind's caress, so much gentler here in the middle of the village. He smells the spicy scent of a pepper tree whose branches hang high over the plaza. Just like all the houses and walls here, the little church is blindingly white, reflecting the sun so brightly you can barely even look at it. The unadorned main entrance bears an announcement in memory of one Don Pedro with a long last name. Above it is an image of Mary, tears of blood running down her cheeks. A mother who has lost her son. She seems to be looking down at Henning.

At the corner of the plaza stands a small grocery. It's closed, but that doesn't make a difference to Henning, since he forgot to bring not only food and water, but money, too. He decides to rest a bit before beginning the trip back. From here to Playa Blanca it's all downhill, so the return trip couldn't take more than an hour. He'll just have to keep his hunger and thirst in check until then. Henning imagines the steep ascent he's just battled morphing into a rapid descent he'll take at breakneck speed. For the first half or so he'll just need to hit the brakes, later on he might need to pedal a little. But it'll be a breeze. He imagines walking back into the apartment and telling Theresa all about his resolutions. How in the New Year he'll laugh more, and be more affectionate with her. How he made it up the steep ascent, all the way to Femés.

Henning lifts his face to the sun and feels its strength. It recharges him like a battery. Pure energy. It won't take long, and soon he'll be good to go.

But as he stands up to get back on his bike,

it becomes clear that's not the case. The aching returns, his muscles cramp up. He holds the handlebars with both hands, and painstakingly places one foot in front of the other, as if he's just learning to walk. Every fiber of his being rises up in resistance at the very thought of riding. No: eating, drinking. That's what he needs to tend to. And maybe even find a place to lie down for a bit.

Pushing the bike, Henning crosses the street, walks through the alley behind the restaurant, and continues a little farther, along a lane parallel to the ridge. To the left and right lie squat houses with small windows, spartan bunkers to ward off sun and wind. They're reminiscent of the era when these mountain folks subsisted on goat cheese, before tourism came to the island. Henning keeps an eye out for any sign of human life, anyone he might ask for help. He tries to remember how you say "food" in Spanish. "Mangiare" is the only thing that comes to mind. If necessary, he can resort to gestures, bringing his hand to his mouth, rubbing his stomach to make himself understood: Hungry. Thirsty. He can get the car, drive back, and pay for everything later this afternoon. But there's no one in sight. Even the gardener and his hose have disappeared; Henning couldn't even say which plot they'd been on. He'll have to knock at one of the houses, on one of the green-painted doors or closed shutters. He just can't decide which. He keeps going, inspecting each facade. This one here looks like nobody's home, that one too, this other one doesn't even have a car in the driveway, and that one over there has an angry dog snarling from its kennel. It's not that Henning lacks the courage to knock, it's just that these are the wrong houses, he's absolutely sure of it.

Bewildered, he finds himself back on the plaza in front of the church, sets his bike down, and slowly turns full circle. There's something here, Henning just isn't sure what. Something that needs to pass. Just as he's wondering whether he's losing his senses out of sheer exhaustion, he notices it. Not a voice, nor a vision, just a direction he has to head in. He takes the bike by the handles and pushes onward. He can't pay any attention to his aching legs right now, he just has to hurry up, before he loses this clear sense of direction. He soon reaches the edge of the village, the lane's asphalt ends, turning into a rocky dirt road. The terrain begins to rise again, heading up toward the flank of Mount Atalaya. No matter, Henning just has to keep going. He climbs around sharp boulders, swerves to avoid big potholes, pulling and dragging the bike more than pushing it. By the roadside he spots a hand-painted sign with a colorful arrow pointing upward: "Artesanía/Art Gallery/Kunst."

I'm climbing yet another mountain, he thinks to himself. What the hell is going on with me? A Sisyphus without his boulder.

As he reaches yet another boulder, behind which the dirt road heads into a curve, he pauses for a short break. He turns around and looks into the valley. The view shocks him. Femés lies far below. Once again he's gone high up without even noticing how. It feels like a cinematic jump-cut. As if some unknown force had simply pushed him 700 feet higher up the mountain. But the eeriest part is that he recognizes what he's looking at. The order of the rooftops, the routes of the lanes, the tiny roundabout in the center of town, he's seen them all before. The angular plaza in front of the church, the little chapel itself, the stout bell tower. He knows this village, from this exact perspective. From above. It's etched into his brain. His bike crashes to the ground next to him; he'd carelessly leaned it against a stony outcrop.

Henning is absolutely certain he hasn't been here over the past few days. None of their excursions have come near Femés. And even if they had, they never would have left town to come up here, following a mountain track made not for shiny rental cars or bikes, but for rickety old pickups with gardening tools rattling in back, for goatherds with spotted flocks, and maybe for the occasional donkey cart. It's hot, scorching hot. The wind has died down completely, as if Henning had entered an entirely different climate zone, a whole new season. A voice recommends he get back on his bike and ride home, drink, eat, rest. Give up this plan, whatever it entails.

He lifts the bike back up and pushes it round the curve, higher up the mountain, along the dirt road. Up above, on a small plateau, a house is nestled into the mountainside. Henning picks up the pace, furiously leaning into the handlebars, as the wheels keep sliding off to the gravelly side. Palm fronds rise above the tall white walls. A terrace overlooks the valley below. There's a towering structure in the middle of the house, vaulted by a glass dome which must cover a large, light-filled hall or courtyard. The dirt road ends in front of the house. So it wasn't a farmer's road, but just a long driveway of sorts, albeit in terrible shape. On the outside wall Henning once again recognizes the same colorful inscription: "Artesanía/ Art Gallery/Kunst."

With a final burst of exertion he reaches the little plateau. Black dots dance before his eyes. He drops the bike and leans against the wall until his lightheadedness passes. His vision is still a little fuzzy, the wind and sun have irritated his eyes, and he isn't wearing sunglasses. He urgently needs to get some shade, to sit down. But he manages to notice a lone car parked in the driveway, a rusty, dark-blue Range Rover. So someone's home. Henning's salvation.

The wrought-iron door is open, he maneuvers his bike inside and stays on the lookout for somewhere to park it. Since he doesn't have a bike lock, he's looking for a hidden spot, even though he can't imagine who would steal a bike all the way up here. He opts to push it out back, behind the house. He leaves the gravel path leading to the wooden double door, and makes his way through palms, mango trees, and bougainvillea to the other side of the yard and around the corner of the house. The space between the house and the outer wall isn't very wide, and looks untended. The twisted branches of a few mimosa trees are filled with litter that must have blown there, and the black gravel on the ground is dusty. Henning's phone vibrates against his tailbone. While he works the bike through the deep gravel with one hand, he wrests the phone from his back pocket with the other. A text message. The display is blackened in the sunlight, he has to get into the shade, he can't make anything out.

It is noticeably cooler in this darker, narrow space. Just as he's about to lean his bike against the outer wall of the house he draws back, aghast. The looming, windowless wall is covered in a sea of spiders. Domed bodies, spindly legs spreading outward like starbursts. Eight-legged suns unevenly arrayed in a bizarre pattern, horrifying in their sheer quantity, even though not a single one is moving, and each, taken on its own, must be harmless. This sight makes Henning recoil even farther back. Deep within him, an alarm sounds. A wailing siren, as unbearable as the screams of a small child. Henning briefly considers the possibility that *it* is coming back, that he's about to endure another attack. But that's not it. Something is rising up from within him, from his most inaccessible, abysmal depths.

He looks at his phone. The text is from Theresa. It says something about calling it quits. Henning has to stare at the spiders. Out of disgust. They shouldn't be there, he has to get rid of them, but how? They're preventing him from understanding Theresa's message. "Dear Henning, we'd best call it quits. It might come as a surprise right now, but I'm certain we'll get through it just fine." She can't possibly mean it. It has to be some kind of joke. He has to get home, talk to Theresa, but the spiders won't let him go. The image of them is burnt into his retina, he can still see them with his eyes closed. He feels sick, dizziness overcomes him, his legs no longer hold him. He lands on his hands and knees, the black gravel digs into his palms. Little pebbles, every single one a miniature boulder, split into crazy bits, none like any other, and all spewed out by the volcanoes that call this place home. Henning falls onto his side, this feeling too is familiar, the pointy, not-entirely-uncomfortable pain of gravel boring into your skin, all over.

"Hey! Hello?"

His head is lifted, his body gently turned. As the rim of a glass touches his lips, he begins gulping the water down. He empties the glass before even opening his eyes. The woman with the French braid. He knows she's not his mother. He isn't hallucinating, he's not going crazy. He knows where he is and what day it is. The ascent, the Range Rover, Theresa's text. The spiders. He turns his head so he can see the wall and has to immediately look away again. They're still there, completely covering the entire surface. Some kind of daddy longlegs, maybe. An infinite number of them.

"They're such a nuisance," the woman says, having followed his gaze. "But they don't do a thing. They don't even come into the house. Do you feel sick?"

He nods and sits up, more easily than he expected.

"You rode up from the El Rubicón plain, didn't you? You must be dehydrated and hypoglycemic. No wonder, given how you're outfitted."

She's wearing an olive-green shirt, washed-out pants of a similar color, and flip-flops on otherwise bare feet with an impeccable dark-violet pedicure. Henning puts her in her mid-fifties.

"Can you stand up?"

She holds him by the arm as he gets up, and doesn't let go as they cross through the garden. The entire front side of the house has a broad terrace, with a wooden double door in the middle, probably the building's main entrance. Henning knows what color the terrace tiles are, even though he can't see them from here. A speckled yellow. The woman doesn't lead him up the stairs to the main entrance, but to the other side of the house, around an addition, to a small blue door at the back of the house. They walk straight into a spacious kitchen. Henning immediately feels better. The room is shady, with just one window over the sink. The thick walls keep it cool. The furniture is built-in, low cupboards, shelves, countertops, plastered smooth and whitewashed, in classic Canary Island style, with rounded corners. It smells of cold olive oil with a faint whiff of onions. In the back part of the kitchen there's a massive wooden table decked out with painting supplies. Tubes and jars in every imaginable color, paint-stained rags, glasses of water containing a pinkish or bluish liquid, used palettes, and a large bowl full of smooth, black, fist-sized stones.

"Have a seat."

The woman pulls a stool over for Henning, and with her forearm sweeps part of the mess over to the other side of the table.

"Behind the main exhibition space I have a

studio, but I do the smaller work here. Now let's get you something to eat."

He watches as she takes a bowl of boiled potatoes and a pair of eggs from the fridge, gets onions, garlic, and olive oil ready, and a skillet, pepper, and salt. Henning tries not to think about the bowl of black round stones, but can't help himself. They're exactly the same as the ones his mother painted. He takes one into his hand and weighs it in his palm. It's real, no doubt. Not imaginary, no hallucination. He's about to eat, and then he'll feel better. Maybe as his lightheadedness passes, the feeling that he knows this place will fade away, too.

"I'm Lisa," the woman says.

"Henning," he replies, quickly adding, "Thank you."

"It's nothing," she laughs. "I'm thrilled to have a visitor. My husband flew to Germany for the holidays. And here I am, sitting around all bored. So coming across a famished cyclist is a treat."

He tries to laugh along, but it sounds forced.

"Where you from, Henning?"

"Göttingen."

"I'm from Hannover, where it's one below, foggy, and sleeting. This your first time on the island?"

"Sure is."

"You like it?"

"Kinda sorta."

"Ah-ha, so you're a kinda-sorta guy."

This time his laugh is real. He likes Lisa. She exudes warmth, and her energy and humor feel good. She seems to enjoy cooking. And she's certainly not someone who would complain about having to do laundry for three. She'd probably hum to herself while hanging clothes up to dry in a sunny courtyard, the next clothespin ready between her teeth, her arms stretching upward. But Henning can also tell Lisa has no kids. He imagines what it would be like to live with her. Up here on the mountain. Linked to the valley only by a steep and rocky dirt road. Beside an older woman who calls him a "kinda-sorta guy" and lets out a friendly laugh. He could reply to Theresa's text: "Agreed. We'll do just fine."

New year, new you.

"Henning?"

His mind has wandered, and he didn't hear Lisa. She's turned from the countertop where everything is laid out and is looking at him quizzically.

"You okay with garlic?"

"Of course."

He grabs his phone and swipes at the screen. It stays dark. Full battery, it must have just shut itself off. Lisa shakes her head.

"Forget about it, there's no service up here," she says as she beats the eggs in a mixing bowl. "No electricity or running water, either. We have an *aljibe*, a type of cistern that collects rainwater. And solar power. Before, there was only a generator. You had to put up with a helicopter-level racket just to turn the lights on. Ah, the price of seclusion."

She points to the window with the mixing spoon.

"The houses down along the Barranco are all new. They weren't there when I bought this place."

Henning nods; somehow he'd already known that, even if he couldn't say how.

"The locals have better connections than we do, getting building permits is no problem for them. Up here, I've been trying to get proper paperwork to make this place aboveboard for years. It's all cronyism. But whatever." She opens her arms wide, mixing spoon in one hand, whisk in the other. "I love this house. More than anything in the world. If you'd like, I'll show you around, after lunch."

"Sure, gladly," Henning replies, even though he really should rush back home. If he even still has a home. He's playing with the black stones again, picking them up from the bowl, giving them a little twirl. They spin like tops, evenly, for a good while. They're perfect ovals, a little flatter than eggs, with tiny pores and a shiny surface, as if they've been polished. They feel good in your hand, making you want to turn them in your palm and caress them. It's a feeling Henning recalls from childhood. He might have more faith and trust in this feeling than in any other.

"You paint these stones?" he asks.

Lisa opens a drawer and brings one to the

table. From its dark surface beams a circular, azure pattern in all tints and shades, from a light baby blue in the middle to an intense dark blue on the outer edge. A mandala made up of dots in varying sizes.

"Nice," Henning says. His mother only paints animals, no abstract patterns.

"You can keep it," Lisa says. "It's not art. But these sell like hotcakes at craft markets. They're the perfect souvenir, a little present from the island, ideal paperweights, doorstops, or murder weapons." She lets out another girlish laugh, tosses her braid back, and Henning thinks he quite likes her. Maybe she has no husband, maybe she just made him up to protect herself from meddlesome men up here in her mountain solitude. "They pay for my paintings. Every now and then I have a show in Playa Blanca or Yaiza, sometimes the honorary consul buys a piece. But usually anything that doesn't feature a sailboat, volcano, or sunset is a tough sell."

She goes back to the stove.

"My mother used to paint stones, too," Henning says, even though he hadn't intended to.

"Oh really?" She turns around again. "What a strange coincidence. In a certain sense the stones are tied to this house. The house gave me the idea. I'll show you how, after, when we do the tour."

As the onions and garlic start sautéing in the oil, Henning is sure he misread Theresa's text message. In a world that smells so splendid, it's unlikely people could commit such acts of cruelty against one another.

With an almost deafening bang, the black stone crashes onto the tile floor, twirls a few more times, and comes to a halt. It slipped from Henning's fingers. Lisa doesn't *tsk*, she lets out a laugh. She's pressing the potato-and-egg mixture between two plates and sliding it onto the skillet. The smell grows stronger, and Henning's mouth waters, a Pavlovian response. Lisa flips the concoction a few times and adjusts the flame, all the while humming a tune Henning recognizes as Ravel's *Boléro*. She sets a bowl of olives, white bread, a glass, and a pitcher of peach nectar on the table. Then a plate, knife, and fork, but no napkin.

"Dig in."

As Henning brings the first bite to his mouth, the taste is so overwhelming he has to close his eyes. He's never tasted anything as delicious as this tortilla. He'll eat the entire thing, but he'll also avoid making a fuss over how tasty it is. He'll chew and swallow every bite until his plate is clean and his stomach is full, even if it might make him nauseous.

Lisa watches without eating anything herself, and smiles with satisfaction at his appetite. She does lift her glass, though, to toast with him. She's not drinking juice, but a chilled liquid that's beaded up with condensation. Henning presumes it's prosecco. In a water glass.

Since he's uncomfortable eating in silence, while being watched, he asks a few questions about the house. Lisa swiftly starts talking. You can tell the house is her favorite subject, and that she's told and retold its history many times before.

Lisa came to the island for the first time back in 1987, ostensibly for a two-week vacation, but then only went back to Germany in order to pack up her previous existence. She discovered the house while on a hike up Atalaya, standing out in its solitude, visible from afar, a somewhat run-down fairy-tale castle. It was empty. She walked right in through the open gate, through the garden, which evidently hadn't been watered for some time, and sat down on the terrace, where a few lawn chairs were still scattered about. She looked out over Femés, the Pozo Valley, the slopes sprinkled with goats. She saw the pearly herons, like white arrows leading the goats along. The reddish canyons, the volcanic peaks of the Ajaches chain. Farther off lay the hazy sea, dotted every now and then by a tiny sailboat. Lisa felt like the queen of the entire earth. She couldn't speak any Spanish. She didn't know anyone on the entire island. Nevertheless, she was able to find out who the house belonged to. And that it was for sale.

"Something had happened here," Lisa said as Henning sopped up the last bit of olive oil from his plate with a bit of bread crust. "It had been rented out as a holiday home, back when it still had no electricity. Then something must've gone terribly wrong, because two little kids were discovered, half-dead, but I never could find out exactly what had happened. But it wasn't any of my business anyway, you know? The house was a real steal."

She finished her prosecco, Henning his juice. He felt heavy and full.

"Over the years I renovated it, built it up a bit, poured tons of love into it. At first I slept here in the kitchen, can you imagine? Then I redid the exhibition space, and later on the bedrooms and art studio. C'mon, I'll show you around."

She brushes her hand against his, and Henning wonders whether she's flirting with him. He still hasn't thanked her for the meal. Lisa ducks into the pantry and refills her glass without offering him anything. Maybe it's prosecco leftover from a lonely New Year's Eve the night before. He props himself against the table with both hands in order to stand up. It's not just his full stomach giving him trouble, now his legs have cramped up, too.

"Once you've set foot here, you never want to leave." They're standing over the sink, which seems to have been carved from one massive block of granite. Lisa isn't much shorter than he. Her braid is woven into a perfect symmetry. It's amazing anyone can manage something like that all on their own. Henning's mother could, too. Once he watched her as she stood in the bathroom, both hands behind her head, her fingers busily weaving. In no time she'd made a tight, even braid that closely followed the contour of her scalp and then loosely cascaded downward. Henning even knows how the braided hair feels on one's fingers. He'd like to touch Lisa's head, carefully glide his hand over the braid's waves, and twirl the free end into a thick coil around his finger. But she'd get the wrong idea.

"My German friends all ask whether there's anything I miss here on the island—cinema, theater, culture. But then every time I'm back with you all, I realize how little films and plays have to offer. You just aren't as lucky as we are here, aren't as happy. You're plagued with worry, so many problems ... Once you've lived here for a while, you just can't relate to all that anymore."

He could tell her about Theresa's message. About a woman who leaves her husband on New Year's Day, by text message, while the kids are playing in the yard of their vacation rental. He could ask her whether that's a real problem, or just a German affinity for worry. But Lisa's a stranger, and he suspects she might say something like, you have to look on the bright side even in a breakup, it's still a chance for something new. Why doesn't he just stay here and start over, the way she did back then?

She leaves through the back door, and Henning follows her on stiff legs. The black gravel covers the whole yard, crisscrossed here and there by thin black irrigation hoses, like endless snakes, all connected to one another. Lisa tells him this ground cover is called *picón*, it comes from the El Rubicón plains, and helps store up water, which is vital to the plants' survival. Henning knows the word. *Prick, pic, picón.* And although he's wearing shoes, he knows exactly how this gravel feels as it pricks the bottom of bare feet.

It's clear this large yard receives great

attention, care, investment, and love. Blooming oleanders, hibiscus, fragrant mallow, fat old cacti, a small palm forest whose fronds produce a steady rustle in the breeze. Off in a corner Lisa has grown an orchard, and names each fruit for him: figs, mulberries, pomegranates, mangoes, papayas, dragon fruits, kiwis, there's nothing that won't grow here. As they walk by a portion of the garden wall, Henning keeps an eye out for more daddy longlegs, but finds none; apparently they only live on that one wall.

Lisa points out additions that could be renovated and rented out as holiday apartments, the garage, and a good spot for a swimming pool, even though she herself prefers swimming in the ocean. She has no desire to rent the place out to tourists, but also no idea how long she'll be able to afford living here. "It's not getting easier, and I'm not getting any younger," she says, looking at him as if she expects him to know exactly what she means.

Next she shows Henning the solar panels and the emergency backup unit, almost as if she were trying to sell the place to him.

Behind the house there's a terrace-like platform, quite large, but with no view, because it's close to the outer wall. It's covered not with tiles, but with a plaster-like layer of concrete. As they step onto the surface, Henning spots the hole. A rectangular cutout in the floor. Large enough to swallow someone whole. Underneath, nothingness, the void. A blackness, an emptiness of the likes found nowhere else on earth. A window into the cosmos. He instinctively grabs Lisa by the arm, as if the hole might draw her in and gobble her up. Or him.

"What is that?"

"That?" She laughs and pats his hand as if to calm him down. "Oh, that's just the old aljibe. An underground cistern. It collects rainwater. Come closer."

Henning haltingly steps up to the edge and peers in. As his eyes get used to the darkness, he can make out the water's surface, maybe twenty-five feet below, pitch black. Lisa grabs a handful of pebbles and drops them in. They make hollow-sounding splashes and ripples appear on the surface, only to swiftly morph back into a black void.

"Is it entirely hollow down there?" He lightly stamps his foot.

"It's a masterful ancient construction, built with barrel vaults. Nothing can break through it. But I only use the aljibe water to irrigate the garden. I had a newer system installed for the indoor plumbing."

"But what would happen if someone fell in?"

"Well, that'd be it." She laughs again. "A cat or two might have vanished down there over the years, sure. But people don't just fall into holes, you know."

She turns to head back toward the house, but Henning stays put, just staring into the void right in front of his feet. He hears a woman's voice: "No way, this can't be! Werner, come here, you have to see this! What if one of the kids fell in? We have to call the landlord, immediately." Then his father's calm voice: "There's no phone here, darling. I'll go find a board to cover it."

"C'mon," Lisa calls out, "I've saved the best for last!"

Henning obeys almost automatically. His brain is no longer sending any conscious commands to his body. His system is on the verge of an emergency shutdown. For a while already he hasn't fully grasped what's going on. He considers the possibility that he isn't even awake, but that's not possible, he knows he isn't dreaming. Nothing makes sense anymore, it's as if the laws of nature no longer applied, as if from one moment to the next he might just lift off from the ground and, lightly spinning, go floating through the garden with Lisa. As if time and space had lost all meaning, and were about to unveil the source code underlying the user interface of life, the cipher connecting every single thing to everything else, revealing a realm in which people are nothing more than points of intersection, nexuses of various energies.

"Forget that pit," Lisa calls over, "over here is where it's at."

They're standing on the front terrace, and the tiles really are speckled yellow. Lisa is lifting the heavy bolt on the towering double door. It's stuck. Henning looks out at Femés. Earlier, that was his end goal, the high point of his journey, and now it lies far below, like a toy village. From here he has an amazing view, and can make out every little detail. He sees concrete mixers in many of the yards, and some houses haven't been refaced in the traditional plaster. Nevertheless it all looks clean and orderly. As Henning takes it all in, the distances seem to shift. The dirt road stretches ever longer, Femés slips farther away, becoming unreachable, and Henning feels as if he's shrinking. The ache in his legs becomes the aching of a little kid's legs, too short to reach anything in the whole wide world.

The bolt gives way.

"Ta-daaa!" Lisa exclaims. She's opened the double doors. Henning peers into the exhibition space. First he sees the stones: a snail, a snake, a scarab, a millipede, all in bright colors, painted in fine dots on the dark background. They're displayed in a brightly lit showcase right next to the entryway. Lisa's voice reaches him from afar.

"These stones aren't for sale. I found them here, they were in the house when I arrived. They're my good-luck stones. They're what led me to this idea."

The middle of the enormous room opens up into a tower of sorts, like a wide shaft, lined with plants trailing down the chains holding up their pots. The top is sealed off by a glass dome through which sunlight cascades.

There are works of art everywhere, paintings, sculptures, but Henning pays them no heed. He looks at the sofa. There it is, pushed toward the corner a bit, adorned in bright, oriental-patterned upholstery. On the sofa sits a woman—no, she's partially reclined, her legs spread, her upper body arched backward. Has Lisa lain down?

But there's the back. The back of a man, naked, triangular, musculature flexed, dark hair growing in two wide swaths on either side of the spine. Has Henning thrust himself onto Lisa? Is he trying to kiss her?

But that's not his back. And that's not Lisa.

IT'S HIS FIRST plane trip. He's so nervous. Where are Mama and Papa? They're looking for a spot to stash their carry-ons in the overhead bins. Papa swears, as usual, when things aren't going the way he wants. And there's Luna, sitting next to Henning, almost jumping for joy in her baby seat. When it's time to fasten her seatbelt, she starts screaming. Mama comes, and bends over him to calm Luna down. Her spicy, sweet smell, her long hair, her warm hands with colorful fingernails, he loves those the most. They have to switch seats, him at the window, Luna in the middle. Then up, up, and away into the sky. Henning couldn't believe they actually went right through the clouds, he figured that was just one of those things grown-ups say. Now he sees it's actually true. He looks down on the clouds from above; they look like a thick layer of snow you could run on top of. Henning imagines how he'd romp around in it, throw cloud-snow up into the air, swirl around in it, make a cloud-snowman. He likes imagining things, to while away the time. The stories in his head are endless. Mama always says he should be thankful for that.

He asks out loud whether they're going to fly to the moon, and his parents laugh.

"You're not entirely off," Papa says. "The island actually does look a little like the moon."

Henning likes making his parents laugh. They like it when he says clever things. Once he said: "The time we have on earth is as tiny as a pebble." Mama hugged and kissed him, and Papa wrote the sentence down and put it on the first page of a photo album. The bit about the pebble came to Henning because he thinks so much about time. He can't read a clock yet, but he often looks at the arrows. You can't see them move, unless you look away and then after a while look back at them. The thing he finds most disturbing about time is that it always goes by too fast or too slow. It never seems to be just right. Henning doesn't believe time is his friend. He said that out loud once, too, and Mama caressed him and hugged him awhile.

In the airplane, time is definitely too slow and too long. They can't get up and run around, and Henning can barely stand staying put anymore. He and Luna bicker. She wants the little fire truck that he got for his birthday and always carries around with him. She tugs on his sleeve and yells, he pushes her away, until Mama tells him he should be nice to his little sister. It's so awful when Luna pokes at him and wants all his stuff and ends up making him angry. She's still mostly a baby, she wears diapers and drinks milk out of a bottle. When she's tired she can be so annoying. But usually she does what Henning says, looks at him in wonder, and is proud when he praises her. Sometimes she says funny stuff like "budda-budda" instead of "butterfly," and he could listen to that all day. "Luna, say 'butterfly'!" And then they both laugh their heads off. Luna likes to laugh more than anything, she has a wide mouth, practically made for laughing. Mama says she's not as serious as he is. But Henning has to be serious, because he's a big boy already. He has to take care of Luna. Even Papa says so. "Henning, look after your little sister for a bit, you're already grown up." "Henning, a big young man doesn't hit his little sister." "Henning, Luna's running off! You need to keep an eye on her." He's often afraid for her. Before they left home, he repeatedly asked if she could fall out of the airplane. Mama and Papa laughed, even though he wasn't kidding this time.

After the flight everything's really confusing, they rush here and there, the suitcases come out on a conveyor belt, the stroller is missing, Mama and Papa run around, Luna falls asleep on top of Mama's jacket on the floor, Henning watches over her even though he's really tired, too. At some point they're sitting in a car, and Henning falls right to sleep. When he wakes up, the car is up on a mountain. Doors bang, the trunk is slammed shut. Henning gets out, runs around the car, and helps Luna, who sometimes falls when she tries to get out of the car by herself. He looks around. Never in his whole life has he ever been this high up. Except in the airplane. It's almost like they're still in the plane.

"Look," he calls out, "down there, the cars!"

"Wi-ddle," Luna says, "tho wi-ddle!"

The cars down in the valley are as little as matchbox cars, and they're driving around along a gray ribbon between the mountains. Henning also discovers tiny houses, tiny palm trees that look like feather dusters, and even a backhoe waving its digger like an arm. Henning can hear the stones rumble, even though it's so far away.

"Papa, they're building a house down there!"

But his parents don't have any time to look, they're carrying in the suitcases and bags. Henning grabs Luna by the hand and they run around behind them.

The house is huge, it reminds Henning of the castles in his books, but it's white, not brown or gray. A broad tower, a big wooden door. The only thing missing is the drawbridge. Inside there's a great big room where the light comes down from above, Henning's never seen anything like it. A bunch of different doors open up onto hallways leading to a bunch of different rooms, you can lose your way like in a labyrinth. But Henning wants to explore the yard, and runs outside with Luna. So that's what it looks like on the moon. There's black gravel everywhere, it crunches under your feet and goes straight into your sandals. Mama said the little black pebbles are called *picón*. Cacti grow here, as tall as grown-ups. The sun burns. They can play knights on horseback here, or pirates, or war, and pretend to run away from home, there are so many options he doesn't even know where to start. There are great hiding places, they crouch under bushes, balance on rickety low walls, Henning holds Luna's hand to make sure she doesn't trip and fall. He's the best brother in the world, Mama says so sometimes when he keeps an especially good eye on Luna.

When she darts off screaming, he rushes over, thinking she's fallen, and asking where it hurts, but she's just standing there on her little-girl legs, crying, and pointing her finger out toward a wall.

"Pider! Pider! Pider!"

Then Henning sees it, too. The entire wall is covered in spiders, they're huge, innumerable, it's worse than anything he's ever seen or dreamt. He picks Luna up and they run off to get Papa, it takes so long to find him, but there he is on the terrace, on a lounger, just smoking a cigarette, and he doesn't want to get up, but they yank on his fingers and yell so much that he finally follows them.

When he sees the spiders, he lets out an astonished sound.

"They're so many, right, Papa?"

"There sure are," Papa says, laying his hand on Henning's head. He holds Luna with his other hand, she's still crying.

"Ulla!" Papa calls out. "Bring the camera!"

Mama comes and takes pictures of the spiders and talks about "marvel" and "motif," as Luna yells "Ge-rid-of-em! Ge-rid-of-em!"

"It's okay sweetie," Papa says, rocking Luna up and down on his arm. "We'll get rid of them."

He goes, and comes back tugging a garden hose. It looks heavy, since Papa seems to strain a bit, but he finally makes it to the wall of spiders.

"Stand back," he says, and turns the jet nozzle on. A stream of water hits the wall and immediately washes a huge wad of spiders down onto the picón. Luna yelps for joy, Henning stares, wide-eyed, and feels like he's about to puke. The water folds the spiders together, sweeps their feet away, and transforms them from big sun-shaped bugs into ugly clumps. Some try to get away, and Papa has fun hunting them with the hose until they get soaked and stream down the wall. They lie on the picón like little handfuls of muck, twisting and turning, trying to wrest their legs free, and Henning can't bear to look any longer. He leaves Papa and Luna's merrymaking and goes into the house.

The next few days are paradise. They go to the beach a few times. Henning builds castles and moats in the warm sand, as Luna sits in a yellow plastic basin Papa has filled with seawater. Or they go for a drive through the otherworldly volcanic landscape. Even with all the car windows open, it's so hot they have to stop after a while and cool off in the shade of an umbrella on the patio of a café, eating ice cream and drinking lemonade.

But they spend most of their time in the house, which is also Henning's favorite place to be. A deep-blue sky stretches out high over the yard, and a light breeze caresses the skin. The rustling palms sound like the surf, and the air always smells of the ocean, too. If you close your eyes, the sun makes circular patterns on your eyelids, and the light makes a kaleidoscopic motion. Little by little Henning and Luna discover every nook and cranny of the yard. The main area they steer clear of is the wall of spiders. They reappeared the very next day, as many as before, a dense pattern of eight-rayed suns covering the house's outer wall. Henning can't tell whether they dried out and climbed right back up, or whether new spiders have taken the place of the drowned ones. Papa doesn't want to bother with the hose again, so there they stay. Henning and Luna just try not to think about them.

And there's another area they avoid. Behind the house there's a cement-covered area, kind of like a patio, but without a table or any lounge chairs. It was actually a perfect place to play tag, but then Mama forbid them from even setting foot on the cement. Because there's a rectangular hole in the middle. When Mama found it, she threw a fit.

"No way, this can't be! Werner, come here, you have to see this! What if one of the kids fell in?"

She grabbed Henning and Luna by the hand and carefully tiptoed over to the edge of the hole. Luna was so afraid of that dark window into the ground that she took teensy steps toward it, leaning far forward. Henning could hardly stand how close she got to the hole. Even though he knew Mama was holding her tight, he still wanted to take her up into his arms and run off to safety.

"A monster lives down there," Mama said, and Henning, who had just been staring down into the darkness, stepped back. He felt a shiver run through his entire body. "If you get too close, it'll pull you in. You mustn't play here, ever. Stay away, got it?"

Papa covered it with a board so the monster wouldn't come out. When Henning and Luna lay in bed at night, Henning couldn't get his mind off it. He feared that the monster lived beneath the entire house, in a basement flooded with water, pitch black and unfathomably deep. Sometimes he heard the monster make noises, a muffled rumble, even though Mama said that was just the wind. He doesn't talk to Luna about it, because he doesn't want to scare her. Their bedroom is already creepy enough. It's completely empty except for two narrow wooden twin beds, which Papa slid together so Henning and Luna could sleep next to each other. Then Papa put two chairs on one side of the bed, so Luna wouldn't fall out at night. The window is small and has bars over it. On the wall there's a picture of a woman looking skyward, crying red tears. As long as Mama is sitting on the edge of the bed each evening, the room is fine. She tells them a bedtime story and pats their heads. The room is comfortably cool, and it's nice and warm under the covers, so Henning feels good. But as soon as Mama leaves, everything changes. The room expands, the walls disappear, the darkness begins to breathe. Luna falls right to sleep, she's always exhausted at the end of the long day. Then Henning lies still next to her, looks at the woman in the picture, and wonders if her crying has anything to do with the monster. If the monster gobbled up her kids, because there aren't any kids in the picture.

When Henning has to go to the bathroom at night, he senses how vast the house is, how thick the walls are, and has to fight to keep himself from calling out for Mama and Papa. During the day he hardly ever loses his way anymore, but at night the house turns back into a labyrinth. Sometimes he manages to find the bathroom without a hitch, but then on the way back can't find their bedroom right away. Then he thinks about Luna, alone in bed under the crying woman, and imagines the monster coming in to get her. When he finally gets back and slides under the covers next to Luna, he's so relieved his head spins.

By morning all these nighttime visions have vanished, the house is bright and clear again, and Henning doesn't even believe in the monster anymore. They have breakfast out on the terrace, fresh-baked croissants that Papa drove into the village to get. It smells like coffee, and every day Mama says that even the early-morning sun is unbelievably strong. And the sun's rays really do warm their faces, even at breakfast. It's so peaceful and glorious.

Over the course of the day Mama and Papa fight a lot. They do that at home in Germany, too. Mama says fighting isn't bad. After all, Henning and Luna yank on each other's hair every once in a while, too, but they still love each other. His parents' fights are something else, but Henning can't quite put his finger on it.

Every other day a man comes to the yard. His name is Noah. He waters the palm trees, trims the hedges, sweeps up fallen flowers. He rakes the black picón until all the kids' footprints are gone. At the very end he works on the irrigation system for a while, connecting thin black hoses to form endless snakes with a ton of little spouts that sprinkle water at the base of all the plants. Henning and Luna crouch down near him and watch. He talks a lot, explains to them what he's doing, but it's in Spanish, so they don't understand a word. Henning knows how to say "hola," "gracias," and "qué tal?" Luna says "sí" and "no," which thrills Noah. At the beginning they were afraid of him, because his voice is so loud and he always has to touch everything. He greets Mama by kissing her on the cheeks, pats Papa on the back, and tosses Luna up in the air. The first time he did it she started to howl, but now she and Henning like Noah a lot, especially when they can't think of what game to play. Sometimes Noah lets Henning hold the hose, and lets Luna throw dried-up flowers into a bucket. Or he puts them both in a wheelbarrow and pushes them in a loop, all the way around the yard.

They have gravel in their shoes all day long. At first they'd yell out "Prick, pic, picón!" and empty out their shoes every few minutes. But then that was too much effort, especially because Luna needs help putting her shoes back on, and Mama doesn't like being called back constantly. So they finally just got used to the little pebbles, and almost don't even feel them anymore. When Mama helps them take their shoes off each night, she finds handfuls of picón. "That's gotta be two kilos!" she exclaims, and goes to the porch to shake it all out.

One time they go to a beach that isn't sand, but black stones. They're smooth and round, and come in all different sizes, little ones like peas, middle ones like goose eggs, big ones like pumpkins. Mama gets excited. She starts collecting the prettiest ones, filling the entire beach bag. The shore has a bunch of little stone towers other tourists have built, some look like men with funny hats gazing out to sea. Papa builds a tower for Henning and Luna, too. The kids gather the best stones, and Papa tries to stack up as many as possible. As he goes, he says words like "balance," "center of gravity," and "stable," words that, to Henning, sound very grown up as he mouths them, a little unwieldy, but good. It's a lovely day. Luna shows off how strong she is carrying stones, Henning plays architect, Papa and Mama are cheerful, and not once does either of them complain that the kids are a bother. The surf drones in the background, breaking on the stones and sometimes splashing up into white fountains. The round stones make a peculiar sound as the water recedes, causing them to roll over one another, like music from a magical instrument. When Henning points it out to Mama, she kisses him and says he has an eye and an ear for beauty. It's as if the black stones emitted some special power.

On the way back Mama insists on stopping at a hardware store to buy paint. They drive across the entire island, it's hot, Luna starts to whine, Papa falls into a foul mood and yells at Luna, which makes her howl even louder. But Mama won't give up until she's gotten the paint she's looking for, plus an assortment of brushes and a small jar of clear lacquer.

Back at the house they sit at the table out on the terrace, and Henning and Luna each get a stone, too. Luna smears so much paint on hers that she's done with it in two minutes, and spreads the rest on the edge of the table and her face. Henning paints a car with red wheels and a blue roof on his stone. Mama dabs bright little dots onto hers, in a bunch of colors, and you can't tell what it is. When Henning asks, she says she's just not done yet, and smiles, and looks really happy.

The next morning at breakfast, the finished stones are on the table, one at each place, and Mama says they're presents. Luna gets a millipede, colorful as a rainbow, she squeals with joy and pushes the stone to her cheeks like it's a stuffed animal. Papa's stone is a snail, and for herself Mama painted a snake. The stone at Henning's place bears a beetle, in gold and other colorful dots, with long feelers and strong legs. At first Henning isn't sure he likes the beetle, but then Mama explains it's called a "scarab" and brings good luck. Henning likes the name, the stone feels delightfully smooth and heavy in his hand. He runs with Luna back to their bedroom, they place the stones on their bedposts, and the room already looks brighter and less sad.

It's an especially hot day. You can already feel the vacation is coming to an end, time is speeding up, each day goes by faster. Despite the heat, Henning and Luna play out in the yard. They work on their snail museum, which they're dead set on finishing. In the shade under a palm tree they've laid out various stones, a couple of round ones from the black stone beach, plus some white ones that break up easily, and brown and black stones with a bunch of holes in them, plus a couple of green ones that glitter in the sun. These stones are the pedestals they set the snail and mussel shells on top of. Pointy, round, small, large, speckled, striped, some that sparkle, some that are all white. As they work, Henning gives instructions. He's the architect, Luna's the assistant. When she's happy, like right now, she chatters to herself nonstop, and everything she says sounds like a question, because she always draws out the last word of every sentence. "Udder 'nail heeeeeer?" Henning likes it when she babbles like that, there's something cheerful about it, like water in a burbling brook, or twittering birds.

At some point it gets too hot, Henning's throat is on fire. Henning says they should go in and see Mama and get a drink.

The double wooden door leads straight from the terrace into the main hall, but the latch is too heavy. To get to the little kitchen door out back, they have to go along the wall of spiders. They hold each other by the hand and run as fast as they can, as fast as Luna's little-girl legs can go through the gravel. Of course Henning would like to go past the spiders a lot faster, but when he starts getting ahead Luna starts shrieking, falls to her knees, and won't go one step further. Then Henning has to go back and pull her up, which is no good, because then he has to go by the spiders a third time in order to go and get Mama.

Cool air envelops them in the kitchen, but nobody's there, so they keep going, through the short corridor and into the main hall, whose entrance is covered by a heavy curtain. "What're we supposed to do in here?" Papa asked the first day, and Mama yelled out, "Dance!" as she spun Henning in circles. Then she sang "Brother, Come and Dance with Me" until they got dizzy.

As Henning battles through the curtain and makes it through, he's blinded by the light pouring down through the dome. But only for a moment—and then he sees the man. He's standing or kneeling or half lying down on the couch with the colorful cover. His back is bare. Henning sees dark hair on either side of the spine, like a road divided into two lanes. He recognizes this back, because Noah sometimes takes his shirt off as he works. Then he sees Mama's legs with the strappy gold sandals he thinks are so pretty, and a bit of her colorful summery blouse, and the end of her blonde braid. The rest of her has somehow disappeared under Noah, who's making weird movements and doing something with his hands, as if he's trying to push Mama deeper into the couch. As Luna starts crying, Noah turns around. He looks at the kids, his mouth hangs open like he wants to call out to them, but by then Henning has already run off. This time he doesn't wait for Luna, even if she's wailing like she's been skewered. He has to get Papa, he knows where to find him and knows he's not supposed to bother him, Papa always gets angry when anyone disturbs his peace, but Henning can't worry about that right now. Papa has to save Mama. Henning runs as fast as his legs will carry him, and as he's running he starts to cry. Papa is on a lounger by the outer wall of the yard, holding one of those fat, funny-smelling cigarettes he rolls himself, and it looks like he's sleeping. Henning yanks on his arm, the cigarette falls to the ground and Papa yells, "Have you gone crazy?" and Henning yells, "Mama! Noah! You have to come!" and Papa grabs him by the shoulders, gets right up close, stares into his eyes, and says, "Calm down! What's happened?" but Henning doesn't know what's happened, he just wants Papa to come, so he wriggles himself loose and runs off, and finally Papa gets to his feet and follows him, winding through all the blossoming bushes, back toward the house.

They're on their way to the back door when the main wooden door up front swings open. Papa turns, Henning follows him, and they both watch as Noah runs across the terrace, and in one go jumps over the balustrade and out into the yard, crashing onto the gravel underfoot. He runs through the palm trees and out to the driveway, where his car is parked. At first Papa plans to chase him, but then they hear Luna shrieking from inside the house, hysterical, like something awful has happened. For the first time in his entire life, Henning sees that Papa is scared. He sees it in his face, his eyes, which grow darker than usual, and in the way he turns his head back. Papa's fear is even worse than his own. Henning is between him and the wooden door, and they go into the main hall together.

What they see is shockingly normal. Mama is holding Luna in her arms, pacing the room and cooing "Shh, shh," as Luna sweats and screams, her puffy little scrunched-up face turning beet red, her hands balled up into fists. Mama's braid is a little mussed up, but her skirt is back over her knees again. She's wearing strappy sandals and her summery blouse and says, "Just a little fall, everything's alright."

Henning knows Luna didn't fall down. She's crying because of what Noah did with Mama. And they saw Noah run off, after all. Henning looks up at Papa and wants to explain that that's not what happened, that he didn't come and get him for no reason, that something really terrible did happen. But Papa looks as if he already knows all that. He stares at Mama. Then he turns around and vanishes. They hear the rental car start up, they hear the gnashing and grinding as the howling engine storms down the dirt road. In the silence that follows, they hear the *whoop-hoop-hoop* of a hoopoe. Normally Mama runs straight out to the terrace to show them the bird with the funny feather headdress. Today she doesn't even seem to hear it. Luna stops crying and looks at Henning as if it's all a game and she doesn't know what to do next. Suddenly Mama comes back to life and says she's going to make lunch. Henning doesn't think it's lunchtime, but he's happy something is happening. The day slowly resumes its course, like a bicycle that rusted up for a bit but now someone's given the pedal a push, so it's getting back in gear. Henning skips out ahead of them and into the kitchen, chanting "We're hungry-hungry-hungry," which normally makes Mama laugh.

But now she's completely silent as she makes tortillas. Henning and Luna are also silent, much better behaved than usual. They don't bicker, don't complain, and Mama doesn't have to tell them to be quiet even once. A delicious scent fills the kitchen, the smell of family and security. They don't eat out on the terrace, but right there in the kitchen. Luna sits on Mama's lap. Nobody says a word. Mama doesn't ask what games the kids played out in the yard. Papa often isn't there for meals, but this time his absence feels different.

The rest of the day goes by like any other, but both Henning and Luna notice that something is off. They can't come up with a game to play together, and as Luna furiously crashes through the snail museum, destroying everything, Henning runs to Mama, howling and desperately clinging to her legs. Then the kids just hang around the kitchen, watching Mama tend to chores, following her into the bathroom, through the main hall, into their parents' bedroom, out onto the terrace, until she gets angry and yells that they should leave her alone for a while. When Henning tells her Luna's diaper is full, she lets out an annoyed sigh, as if changing diapers were the worst thing in the world.

Henning grabs a couple of books they brought with them from Germany and sits out on the terrace, in the shade. Luna comes over to him, they flip through the well-worn pages together, and Luna yelps with joy when she can point to something. "Where's the cat?"

"Theeere!"

They pass the time.

And then they hear an engine, see the rental car, Papa steps out. They run over to him, throw themselves into his arms, and he lifts them up and hugs them close, tightly, kissing the hair on their heads, rocking them back and forth, and then spinning each of them in a circle a few times, which they really love.

They run ahead of him back into the house, "Mama, Papa's back!" but Mama doesn't come out onto the terrace, she's inside somewhere, so they go to find her and as they come into the kitchen she looks like she's been crying. Their parents don't say hi, they just look at each other silently and send the kids outside.

Henning and Luna go back to the terrace. Mama and Papa shout at each other, but you can't understand what they're saying. The books have lost all their magic, now they're just a bunch of old pages that Luna has torn almost all the corners from. At some point they're called in to dinner. It's just white bread and bologna and a few hardboiled eggs. Henning can hardly eat a thing, and nobody says a word. If there had been a clock in the kitchen, you'd have heard it ticking the entire time.

Right after dinner Mama puts Henning and Luna to bed, even though they aren't tired. She sits on the edge of the bed and looks at them both. Henning is holding her hand and doesn't want to let go, he wants her to sit there the whole night. He begs her to tell a bedtime story, but Mama says she's not in the mood. She says they have nothing to worry about. Everything will work out with Papa. Even grown-ups have dumb fights sometimes, but the important thing is that they make up and stick together. Henning nods in agreement. When he fights with Mama or Luna, it's like his whole body is being torn apart, and it hurts so much he can barely stand it. But then when they make up again, the tear heals, and a warm feeling fills him from head to toe. He tells Mama, and she covers his face with little kisses. She gives Luna a bunch of kisses, too, and says everything will be okay.

But then neither of them can sleep for quite some time. Henning doesn't feel like he can go to Mama and Papa's bedroom, even though he doesn't hear any more yelling. He and Luna grab their painted stones and bring them to bed, Luna is the millipede and Henning is the scarab, and both insects crawl over the blankets, going for walks, fighting, making up, saving one another from holes that monsters live in, until Luna falls asleep.

The next morning Mama and Papa are gone.

Henning gets up while Luna is still sleeping. He runs down the corridors, which have now shrunk down to their usual length, and into the sun-drenched main hall. As usual, the big wooden door is open to let the fresh morning air in. He walks onward to the kitchen, where it usually smells sweet in the morning, and a little bitter from coffee, as Mama stands at the sink washing the dishes or preparing breakfast.

But nobody is in the kitchen, and it doesn't smell like anything. So Mama and Papa must be out on the terrace. Henning runs back through the main hall, his bare feet pitter-pattering against the cool floor tiles. He runs through the main door and outside, where it's very warm and so bright he can't see a thing. He walks along the balustrade and across the entire terrace, which on one side is protected from the wind by a wall, and from the sun by a wooden roof. That's where the big built-in table and benches are, where they usually eat breakfast.

The table is empty. Mama and Papa are nowhere in sight.

Henning hears the hoopoe. He hears the wind in the palms, a sound like rain on the top of a tent. He feels the ground under his feet, and the first few pebbles of the day, which are already pushing into his soles. Maybe his parents are still sleeping. Sometimes Henning wakes up too early. When that happens in the summertime, it's already light but the world still seems deserted. But he doesn't think that's what's happening today. He can guess how late it is from the color of the light. He looks at the sky, the sun, and the yard. It isn't sleeping time, it's already the colors of breakfast time. He heads for his parents' bedroom anyway, which is to the right of the main hall, in a part Papa calls the "west wing." Another corridor, more doors, another bathroom. Henning just wants to peek, he doesn't want to disturb them, and he won't climb into Mama's side of the bed like he sometimes does after he's had a bad dream, oh so quietly so as not to wake Papa. Their bedroom door is ajar. Henning pokes his head through the crack. The room is bright, the curtains are open, the bed is made. Henning is relieved— so they've already gotten up, they must be in the bathroom, and you can't interrupt them in there.

He goes back to the kitchen, sits down at the big wooden table, and waits. A couple of round, black stones are on the tabletop in front of him, one has bright green and red dots on it, but you can't yet tell what it's going to be. Various brushes are laid out neatly on a piece of parchment paper. There's a glass half full of water that's tinted an undefinable color. The paint-covered palette, various tubes. Henning likes the smell of the paints. He knows he's not supposed to touch anything, but still sticks his nose into a paint-stained rag. It smells like Mama, and makes him feel a little dizzy.

When he can't sit any longer, he runs through the house again. He doesn't hear a thing, no shower running, no toothbrushing, no razor buzzing, not even Papa's loud snort as he blows his nose each morning. He goes back to the kids' bedroom, where Luna is lying on her back, legs up in the air, kicking, talking to herself. She has her millipede in hand, and tosses it up in the air. When she sees Henning she says "Hello." He stands still in the middle of the room. Luna looks like she always does. Everything looks like it always does. But he doesn't know what he should do now. Normally he'd take Luna by the hand and they'd go out to the terrace, where Papa would put her on his lap. Henning would climb up onto the bench next to Mama, and they'd all have breakfast together. As he thinks about breakfast, his stomach grumbles, he's really hungry.

He lies next to Luna and they play with their stones for a while, until Luna scrunches up her face and says "Eat!" Her hunger always comes on strong and sudden. And then, if she doesn't get something to eat right away, she can throw a terrific tantrum.

As they scramble down out of bed, he helps so she doesn't fall. She runs out ahead of him, down the corridor, through the main hall, and through the wood door onto the terrace, she knows the way just as well as he does, and her feet make the same pitter-patter sound. Watching her run in front of him, Henning is certain that Mama and Papa are sitting outside, that everything is normal, that they'll say, "There you two are, finally!" as they round the corner.

The terrace is empty.

"Where Mama? Where Papa?" asks Luna.

"I don't know," says Henning. He feels like he's about to cry.

Luna runs back into the house like she's on a mission. He follows, a bit slower, and catches up to her in the kitchen. She asks for Mama again, and he says Mama will be right back.

Now he notices something he'd overlooked before. There are things on the floor. A broken glass in a red puddle, it's wine, he can smell it. The leftovers from dinner are on the counter next to the sink, the milk and cheese weren't put back into the fridge. And things were lying around in his parents' bedroom, too, the dresser was open, there were some clothes on the floor. Mama always keeps things tidy, it's important to her. When the kids don't put away their toys, she gets angry.

"Don't go near there," Henning says, pointing to the shards of glass. And because she doesn't understand him, he takes her by the hand and leads her right up to the puddle. "There, ouchie! Ouchie!" he says, pointing to the shards again.

"Ouchie! Ouchie!" Luna repeats, also pointing to the puddle on the floor.

Suddenly the day comes to a standstill. Henning dips a toe into the wine and draws circles on the floor. The sun shines in through the window, a flock of sparrows chirps in one of the palm trees. It's like nothing will ever change, as if there will never be anything to do. When Luna wants to copy what he's doing with the wine, he says no, and the day moves onward. He leads Luna out of the kitchen.

"Let's look for Mama," he says.

He's got an idea. Maybe he and Luna slept so long that their parents already finished breakfast. Mama's out for a walk and Papa's sitting on a lawn chair near the outer wall with one of his extra-thick cigarettes. Out on the terrace, Henning puts his shoes on. He's not really supposed to run around outside in his pajamas, but he figures today can be an exception. Then there's another problem. Luna doesn't want help putting her shoes on. When he picks up one of her shoes, she yells "Mine!" and grabs it from him.

"You have to put them on," Henning says. "We're going to look for Mama. Gravel ouchie on feet."

Luna sulks. They wrangle over the shoe a little while, until Henning gives up.

"Then just go barefoot," he says.

Luna cheers and waddles after him. When she makes it down the little stairs and sets one foot onto the gravel, her face scrunches up.

"Ouchie!" she says.

"See?" Henning says. "Told you so."

Luna sinks down onto her knees in the

gravel at the foot of the stairs and folds her arms. That means she won't budge.

"Fine," says Henning. "I'm going to look for Mama."

He's hardly gotten anywhere when she starts screaming. He keeps walking. She screams louder. After just ten steps she's crying and howling at the top of her lungs. Her face is red, tears are streaming from her eyes, her huge mouth is warped into a crooked grimace. To Henning it looks like a bad belly-ache, like when you're about to puke. He goes back, kneels down, and takes her in his arms. Her sadness is as vast as the universe. He rocks her back and forth, and wants to cry as well, but he can't, as long as he's holding Luna.

"Shh, shh," he says, just like Mama always does. "Shh, shh."

After they've crouched there for a while, Henning has another idea.

"Wait here!" he says, and jumps up. Luna immediately stops crying and smiles at him. She's understood. Henning is going to get something, and she should wait. Usually something exciting happens next, a new game, or some other discovery.

Henning runs across the terrace and into the house. It feels good to have a plan. It feels good to run! He returns with a pair of Luna's socks, the thickest ones he could find. Together, they manage to pull the socks onto her feet. So Luna can walk on the gravel. She's gobsmacked, and runs out into the yard.

As Luna runs, she counts "two, three, four" and "seven, eight, nine" and then yells "Here I come!" just like she learned playing hide-and-seek. She thinks it's a game, and maybe it is. Henning decides to just count along, from one to ten, then recites, "Ready or not, here I come!" They run around the yard together, and find Papa's lawn chair. "No Papa here," Luna says. They find the spot where Mama sometimes looks out over the wall down into the valley, they even go by the wall of spiders and over the concrete area, where the monster is lurking in the water deep below. Henning tries not to look at the board covering the hole, as if it could pop up at any second. He doesn't know what would peer out.

After they've run around the whole yard, Luna stops counting and starts whimpering. Henning wants to keep going, calling out louder, "seven, eight, nine," and "Ready or not, here I come!" He takes Luna by the hand and tries to encourage her to run with him. He doesn't want the game to end. If the game ends, it means there's a final score, and he can't stand the implication. It would mean the final score is nil–nil—they've found neither Mama nor Papa.

The sun is too strong. Luna can't go on. She wrenches her hand out of his, and grumbles to herself.

"Okay," Henning says. "We'll go inside. Mama must be in there again by now."

"Yeah!" Luna yelps, and runs off with renewed energy.

As they get to the steps leading back up to the terrace, Henning notices something: the car is gone. At that spot, the wall enclosing the yard is low, and has a gate that's always open. On the other side lies the driveway, where the car is usually parked, and then the dirt road leading down to the village, so full of potholes and rocks that when the car drives down it, the hood bumps up and down like a ship on the open sea. That makes Henning and Luna squeal from the back seat, in a mixture of excitement and fear.

In order to be absolutely certain, Henning runs through the gate to the driveway and looks around. As usual, the view virtually jumps at him, the mountains so huge they're actually too high to see. But he sees them, a pale brown and black, and the blue sky above. In some spots the mountains have steps like on a big staircase, in others it looks like massive worms are wriggling around on them. On one of the slopes he spots a swarm of black-brown dots, a herd of goats grazing on the parched grasses. The white dots around them are pearly herons, Mama explained that they sometimes even ride on the goats' backs. Down in the valley, the village is teensy but he can still hear all its sounds, hammering, barking dogs, car engines, and the occasional baby crying. The driveway is definitely empty.

"Look, Luna!" Henning calls out. "The car is gone!"

She runs up behind him. In high spirits,

he grabs her hands and whirls her in a circle.

"The car is gone, the car is gone," he sings to the tune of the children's song "The Rooster is Dead." Luna doesn't understand, but she's happy he's dancing with her.

"Mama and Papa are in Femés," Henning explains. "They're getting croissants for breakfast!"

"Breaaakfaaast!" Luna yells. She laughs and runs toward the house, and now Henning notices how hungry he is, too.

Back in the kitchen they decide to surprise Mama and Papa by getting the breakfast table ready. First, tidying up. Henning carefully picks up the shards of broken glass on the floor and tosses them into the garbage. He tries to wipe up the wine, too, and gets a little scared when the towel turns red. Hopefully mama won't be upset. Usually she's nice and understanding when she knows he was just trying to help. He pulls open the utensil drawer and finds everything straightaway. Luna loves setting the table. He hands her a spoon, and she runs right off, down the corridor, across the main hall, through the wooden door, and onto the terrace, where she sets the spoon onto the built-in table. Then she runs back, he hears her footsteps on the tiles, and how she falls because it's so slippery in stocking feet. She comes, gets the next spoon, and runs off again, taking every piece one at a time, fully concentrated on the task at hand. Henning counts out the plates, and double checks with his fingers—Mama, Papa, Luna, he almost forgot to include himself, four plates, so the stack is pretty heavy. He can't reach the breadbox on his own, even on his tippy-toes, so he needs a chair. Mama doesn't like it when the kids climb around the kitchen, but he figures today can be an exception for this, too. He finds a croissant and half a baguette from the day before, and takes them out just in case the croissants Mama and Papa are getting in Femés aren't enough. And anyway, Mama always says even old bread has to be eaten. He takes butter and marmalade out of the fridge, gets the tray from the sideboard, puts it on the floor, and sets everything on it. It's too heavy to carry. Luna comes over, sees the baguette, and grabs it. He goes to grab it back, "We're about to have breakfast, you've gotta wait," but she shrieks, bites into the bread, and runs off before he can get it back.

"You're such a pain! We're still setting the table!"

He easily catches up, since he's so much faster. She seriously doesn't want to let go of the bread, holding on with both arms, screaming, kicking, and thrashing while still managing to bite into it. When Henning yanks at it, it tears apart, and Luna falls backwards. She just sits and keeps eating.

"You're such a pain."

Henning starts crying. Mama hates it when they nibble on anything right before mealtime. He feels that, if they don't manage to get the breakfast table ready, there won't be any breakfast. And then Mama and Papa won't come back.

Despite that, he sinks to the floor next to Luna and devours the torn bit of baguette. He's that hungry. Maybe they don't even have to tell Mama, maybe she won't even notice. His tears make the bread taste salty. Luna looks happy as she eats. When she notices how hard he's crying, she goes onto all fours, crawls toward him, then stands up and, wide-eyed, stares straight at him.

"You're such a pain," Henning sobs.

She offers him her piece, but he shakes his head and pushes her hand away. They eat in silence. Luna's diaper reeks; Mama will take care of it as soon as she's back.

Once they've finished, Henning's tears have dried up and he feels a bit better. Ultimately, nothing has really happened. They took the bread, but they're still setting the table. Mama and Papa will come back any time now. Luna helps him bring everything out to the table, staying close by his side and asking over and over if he feels better, and he says "Uh-huh, yup, all better," over and over, because Luna won't let up.

The breakfast table doesn't look exactly the way it does when Mama sets it, but Henning is proud of his work all the same. He considers getting a couple of flowers to decorate the table, but isn't sure he should pick any from the blossoming bushes without getting permission first. They sit down at their places and wait.

Luna plays with her utensils and drums her spoon on the stone tabletop. Otherwise it's completely quiet. They see a cat slinking along the garden wall, Henning points and Luna yells, "A gat! A gat!"

After a while Henning says, "C'mon, let's go see if we can spot the car yet."

Luna runs off ahead of him and down the steps, so fast that for a moment Henning is afraid she'll fall, but she zooms off across the yard and onto the driveway.

The mountains are silent. The sky is silent. The dirt road winds down toward the valley. The sound of hammering and barking dogs drifts up from the village.

Luna asks after Mama and Papa. Henning says, "They're on their way."

They go back to the terrace. They wait at the fully set breakfast table. They run back out to the driveway, and wait some more. The sun is high in the sky. The hoopoe swings by and sings *whoop-hoop-hoop*. Now and then Henning spots an airplane, fairly low, about to land on the island. He tries to imagine all the people in the plane, families peering out the window, kids coloring with crayons, eating a snack, just like they did on the flight there. It doesn't seem possible. Even the sounds coming from Femés seem impossible, the little cars driving around on the winding ribbon of the road seem unreal.

Before they flew to Lanzarote, they'd gone with Mama into the city a few times, to the Christmas market, where they'd eaten roasted chestnuts and then bought gifts. The shop windows framed entire toy landscapes. Model trains chugging through forests, fields, and towns. There was a construction site made of Legos, and all the cars and trucks and cranes moved. A Playmobil fire truck with firefighters, pumps, hoses, and hydrants. You couldn't touch anything or play with any of it. You could only look. Everything ran its course, in loops, whether Henning and Luna were there or not. None of the little figurines turned their heads to look at them. That's how the world looks to him: a place where everything is moving, but on the other side of a windowpane.

They sit back down on the terrace. At some point Luna starts whimpering.

"Mommy?"

"Mommy's coming."

"Mommy?"

"She's coming!"

Luna won't stop. She's kneeling on the bench, has laid her head down on the cool stone tabletop, runs her fingers along the edge of her empty plate, and whimpers. Mommy, Mommy. For Henning her whining is like a sword piercing his heart, twisting and turning, making the wound wider and wider. The pain grows until he can't help but yell, "Shut up!" and then Luna yells, too, "Thirs-theee, thirs-theee." Henning isn't sure what she's saying, but he's relieved it's no longer "Mommy." His anger fades. He goes over to her, softly pats her back, and asks, "What's that? What's up? What do you want?" just like Mama would. Normally he doesn't like to hug Luna, she's always covered in drool or spittle, and she fidgets, hitting Henning in the head or on his chest. But now he tries to get ahold of her arms, but she pushes him away and yells "Thirs-theee" again, as if he's taken something from her.

"Are you thirsty?"

"Yeaaah!" she howls.

So that's it! Henning notices how his throat is burning, too. They're thirsty. Thirst is the problem.

"C'mon, quick, into the kitchen!" he says.

They run into the house, Luna is happy because she's about to get something to drink, and Henning is happy, because she's stopped whining.

The carafe is on the sideboard. Henning gets a chair. He can definitely make another exception for this. When he gets up onto the chair he realizes he's forgotten the glass, so he climbs back down. He doesn't know where the glasses are, but finally finds them on a shelf against the wall; it's too high up, he can already tell, he doesn't even need to try. Fright sets in and shakes him. No glass, no water. No water, no quenching their thirst.

"We need a glass, Luna."

"Glass, glass, glass!" She hops up and down, pointing to something, and it takes him a minute to understand. She's pointing to the sink, where the dish rack is, including four glasses.

"Oh, Luna! You're so smart!"

He's proud of her, and hugs her tight, if only for a moment, because she's stomping with joy, because she's done something right. Sometimes Papa tells Henning he's smart when they talk about the universe and Henning knows the difference between stars and planets, and can explain what a galaxy is. He pushes the chair over, climbs up, gets a glass, pushes the chair again, sets the glass next to the carafe, climbs up the chair, and picks up the carafe with both hands. It's heavy and wet, covered in water droplets, and slips out of his hands, falls onto the sideboard, sprays water everywhere, and slides from the sideboard to the floor, landing with a massive bang, spinning around and spilling more water, until it comes to a halt in the middle of a puddle. Luna and Henning freeze in fear, agape with dread. If Mama and Papa heard that, they'll be so angry!

The crash dies away, the house is silent. It occurs to Henning that Mama and Papa aren't even there. They can't have heard anything. For half a second he's happy about that.

"It's not so bad," he says to Luna. "Nothing's broken."

Luna repeats his words.

"We have to wipe up," Henning says.

He picks up the empty carafe and sets it on

the table. What he needs is a towel. The kitchen towel is still wet and red with wine; Henning doesn't know where the clean towels are. He's wary of taking one from the bathroom. He starts randomly pulling open drawers, goes into the pantry, opens cabinets, looks on the shelves. While he's looking, Luna starts whimpering again, "Thirstheee, thirs-theee." But Henning has to wipe up. He spilled something, and he has to clean up after himself, or else Papa will look at him and say, "What's this?" in a weird voice that Henning can't stand. Henning is a big boy, a good brother, a sensible child. If he doesn't wipe up the puddle, Mama and Papa won't come back. His legs are wet, it almost feels like he peed his pants. He looks down and sees he's still in his pajamas. Luna is, too. They have to change, they can't just run around in their pajamas all day, if they don't get dressed then Mama and Papa definitely won't come back. Luna has started romping around in the puddle in her stocking feet, he yells, "Luna, don't!" and she slips, "See?" Henning shouts, but Luna is screaming much louder, she can't even hear him, she's hurt her elbow. Because she won't get up, he pulls her across the floor by her arm, her socks are soaked through, her pajamas, too, they're getting water all over the kitchen, he keeps pulling as Luna keeps screaming, out into the corridor, where she finally stands up, gives him her hand, and follows him, howling.

Under the bed of the room they're sleeping in is a big suitcase full of their clothes. "Your closet," Mama jokes as she pulls it out. Luna wants to take everything out all at once, but Henning stops her. He finds shorts and a T-shirt for himself, a little dress for Luna, clean socks, too, and lays it all out on the bed, it looks good, nice and organized. He quickly takes his pajamas off and puts his clothes on, no problem, he hasn't needed help for a long time now. Luna watches. Henning tells himself he knows how to dress Luna, too. He's watched Mama do it a hundred times. He says, "Arms up!" and Luna obediently raises her arms. With a little tugging and pulling he manages to get her pajama top off. He says, "Sit back!" and Luna sits back and stretches her little legs toward him so he can pull off her pajama bottoms. He even gets the wet socks off her feet. Then he smells it.

"Did you go poo-poo?"

Luna shakes her head. When she shakes her head, her diaper is full.

"Mama will do that when she's back, okay?"

Luna starts pulling at her diaper, one side is already open, "Wait, stop," says Henning, and gets her to lie on her back. He pulls at the tape until it opens up, and then he sees the mess. Luna pooped, and it's awfully liquid. It's all over her bum, her legs, even her back.

Luna sticks her hands out, the way Mama has taught her to. He kneels before her, motionless. He doesn't know what to do. He has absolutely no idea. This is worse than the puddle of water, a lot worse. Wet wipes, he needs wet wipes. They're in the bathroom.

"Wait here, got it? Don't get up! Wait!"

He runs as fast as he can, and to him it seems he has only been away for a second, but Luna has gotten up anyway. Her diaper has fallen to the floor, dirty side down. As he starts to wail, she sits back down on it. Poop is everywhere, it smells horrific, and as

Henning tries to wipe it up he's only spreading it, not getting rid of it. He's crying so hard he can barely see. And then he stops wiping and just sits and wails. Luna has grabbed a few wet wipes, too, and is wiping the poop around. She isn't crying, she's completely quiet. Henning cries until he can't anymore. He hears the hum of an airplane, far in the distance. The palms rustling outside the window. Not a peep from the hoopoe.

It's so quiet that Henning's thoughts begin to wander. He sees Noah on top of Mama. Then Papa came, and Noah ran away. Later, Papa drove off, then he came back. Did Noah steal something? Did Papa drive off to look for him?

Mama was fine. Nothing had happened to her.

Are they both out hunting Noah now?

No, Henning thinks, Noah's no thief. He pushed him and Luna around in the wheelbarrow, and thieves don't do things like that.

Henning notices how happy he is that the car is gone. Because it means that Mama and Papa are in the car. That's good, even though he doesn't know where the car is. Suddenly an idea comes to him.

"Luna," he says, "they must just be lost!" He laughs. "Mama always says she can never find the way, right? She says she has no sense of direction."

"Eck-shun?"

"She says, if she were a bird, she'd never find her own nest." He laughs again. He likes it when Mama talks about herself like that. "Papa must've let her drive to get croissants. And then they got lost. And now they can't find the house. But at some point Papa will drive, and he knows the way home."

"Papa?"

"Later," says Henning. "They'll come a little later. We just have to wait."

"Luna waits," Luna says, and it sounds so sensible that he'd give her a big hug again, if she weren't so filthy. He runs into the bathroom and gets the biggest towel he can find. Back in their bedroom, he leads Luna off to the side and puts the towel on the floor, over the dirty wet wipes, on top of the brown splotches and streaks, he covers it all up and stretches the towel out as flat as he can. It looks okay, and even the smell isn't as bad. When Mama and Papa come back, they won't see it right away, and then he'll have a chance to explain what happened. He cleans Luna's legs with fresh wet wipes, wipes her fingers, and pulls the dress down over her head. Now Luna looks normal again. He sticks the dirty wet wipes under the towel. You can't toss them in the toilet, that's very important, Mama always repeats that. Otherwise it'll clog. Henning thinks that in reality it's just that the monster doesn't like wet wipes. It would get angry if you tossed anything like that down there.

"Thirs-theee," says Luna.

Water. He completely forgot. They run back to the kitchen, and Henning is proud of Luna's little dress, and the fact they're both wearing proper clothes. The puddle on the floor is a lot smaller than he remembered, and you can even see how it'll dry up all by itself. Another relief. It's almost as if the poopy mess in the bedroom never even happened. Mama and Papa will come back.

The carafe is empty. The canister they get water from the supermarket in is way too heavy. As a joke, Papa let him try to carry it once; that's how he knows he can't do it.

"Thirs-theee," says Luna, pointing at the faucet over the sink. Henning can open it. He can, for example, climb up on a chair and wash his hands, all by himself, with soap and everything. He could set a glass under the faucet and fill it up. But that won't work. You can't drink the tap water, that's another thing Mama has said a million times, especially to Luna when she's in the bathtub playing tea party. She talks to herself the entire time, scoops water up in a little plastic cup, and drinks from it. Mama has forbidden it.

"Not here," Henning says. "The water here isn't like the water at home. If you drink it, you'll get sick."

Of course Henning knows why, too. Underneath this house, the monster sits and pees in the water. Monster pee-pee is poisonous. You can die from it.

But you can also die if you don't drink anything. Mama always says that, when he's sick and doesn't want to drink anything because his throat hurts so bad.

"It's okay if you don't eat, but you have to drink. And drink a lot. If you don't drink at all, you die."

Henning looks at Luna. She's crying again, pointing to the faucet and holding her throat. Henning's throat hurts, too. He imagines Luna dying because she hasn't had anything to drink. He imagines her lying on the floor and turning into a lifeless pile, like the dead animals on the side of the road. He feels nothing. He thinks, at least then she wouldn't whimper and whine anymore. But when Mama and Papa found little Luna lying on the tiles, dead, they would go away again. Or not even come back in the first place.

Suddenly Henning has a great idea. He has great thoughts a lot, sometimes even Papa tells him so.

"Wait!" he says, and runs all the way to their parents' bedroom. Sometimes there's a glass of water on their nightstand, next to the little box with Mama's pills, which he's strictly forbidden from touching. And he's in luck. The glass of water is half-full. He picks it up with both hands and slowly walks back, very carefully balancing it so as not to spill a drop. He offers it to Luna, who grabs it from his hands.

"Slow, slow," he says, but she's already gulping, chugging it down.

"I want some, too," says Henning. "We're sharing."

But Luna doesn't stop, and won't let go of the glass. As Henning tries to take it from her, it falls and rolls across the floor, spilling the rest. The unfairness of it tears a hole in Henning that hurts so bad. And through this hole an evil burst of anger emerges. It takes Henning's hands and lashes out at Luna.

"That was our water! I wanted some, too!"

His hands strike Luna, pushing her so hard that she falls backwards and hits the floor. The second she starts crying, and just lies there, the hole closes up. The evil anger is gone. Henning kneels down next to Luna and strokes her back.

"It's okay. I wasn't even all that thirsty."

And because he knows he can't do anything to calm her down, he leaves her lying there. With Luna sometimes you just have to wait, that's what Mama has said, too. And anyway, another great idea has just come to him. The fridge! He hadn't even thought about the fridge. The fridge is off-limits, Papa says. If they need something, they should ask. But this is another exception. Henning can picture it: Mama will explain to Papa that they needed something to drink. That Luna drank the rest of the glass herself and that Henning needed some, too. Papa nods, "Okay," he gets it.

Henning grabs the handle with both hands and pulls. He has to use his whole body to yank backwards, until the door opens with a smacking sound. There's an opened container of orange juice inside. They usually only get one glass of that, on Sundays, at breakfast. The juice is expensive. Henning twists the cap off, lifts the container with both hands, and drinks. No glass, no inhibitions. Drinking juice makes you happy. It pours like light down your throat. Henning keeps drinking, and when Luna comes over he hands her the container, no fuss, and she finishes it.

"Yummy," she says, and they laugh.

They kneel together in front of the open

fridge. There's an opened jar of black olives, which Henning loves and Luna hates. A few nectarines, which are quick to spoil if you don't keep them in the fridge. Some ham, cheese, tomatoes. Some more veggies, and even a bar of chocolate.

Luna grabs at it. Henning doesn't stop her. She stuffs her mouth with chocolate until brown drool drips down her chin. Henning takes just one square, then goes for the ham. No plate, no bread. He shoves it all in, it's like a party, a birthday or Christmas, when other rules apply, when you get presents and can stay up late. They laugh as they eat, and then when they're so full they can't take another bite, Henning grabs Luna by the hand and just barely remembers to close the fridge door before they run off into the main hall, climb up on the couch and jump up and down like it's a trampoline, until the color-ful cover falls to the floor and they're totally out of breath. They run to their parents' bed-room and jump up and down on the big bed. Luna opens the wardrobe and takes out Mama's shoes, the pairs she loves, the white ones with sparkly beads and the red ones with high heels. She sticks her little feet in and shuffles around the room while Henning tosses Papa's underwear into the air, one pair after another. "Look, birds," he yells, as a quiet voice tells him they're not allowed to do any of this, it's bad behavior, but instead of listening to the voice he turns rolled-up socks into cannonballs, plays catapult, *ka-blam*, *ka-blam*, and Luna nearly laughs herself to death as two of the socks hit the ceiling lamp, which begins to swing as Henning says "Whoops!" He pulls Papa's shoes out and flings them onto the bed, puts one of his undershirts on his head, and pretends a pair of jeans is strangling him like a snake with its legs. Luna laughs. They pull Mama's dresses off the hangers and an ocean of flowers, bows, and colorful stripes spreads out across the floor. They throw Mama's underwear around the room, even her bras, and even though Henning feels a little pain about what they're doing, they just keep going.

Then the fun is over. Their laughter ebbs and won't come back, Henning tries to laugh again, once, twice, but it sounds forced, fake.

The sudden silence feels like a verdict, like when Mama doesn't swear, but stays silent, and the silence is so much worse. They lie on the bed, Henning closes his eyes so he doesn't have to look at what a mess they've made. His head doesn't really have any thoughts anymore, just a bunch of jumbled images. He sees Noah's back and Papa's mustache. He sees the yard and the garden and the hoopoe and the shells of the snail museum. And even though he keeps his eyes closed, he sees the chaos in their parents' bedroom, Luna's poop and the remains of their meal strewn out in front of the fridge. He sees Mama's loving face, her beautiful long hair, and how she smiles when she bends down toward him. Now he knows they won't come back. Ever.

Henning talks to the universe. He promises the universe he'll do anything, if only it'll bring his parents back. He'll always be a good boy, and he'll never make Luna angry. He'll clean his room, won't dawdle when it's time to get in the car, and won't ask for another ice cream after dessert. He imagines Mama and Papa running across the yard, calling out, "Sorry we were away for so long, darling," and "What a good job you did looking after your sister! You're such a big boy!" and Papa will toss Luna into the air, and Luna will whoop with joy.

He wants to get up and go back to waiting again. If he doesn't wait, Mama and Papa won't come back. He struggles to sit up, and sees that Luna has fallen asleep. For a few seconds he panics, Luna almost looks dead she's lying so still, and Henning is awake and all alone. He senses that he cannot exist without her. Without Luna, everything ceases to be. When she just lies there, not moving, Henning has no idea what he's supposed to do next.

Just as he's about to wake her, a word pops into his mind: nap! Of course, this is naptime. They nap every day. Mama insists on it, even when they put up a fight. Usually Luna falls asleep quickly, but Henning doesn't, he hasn't taken a real nap for a long time now. That's why he's allowed to bring a couple of books to bed with him, so he can lie there looking at pictures until Mama comes and saves him from the excruciating boredom.

Luna is napping, that's good. Mama will be thrilled that Henning remembered naptime! And how he got her into bed so quickly. No drama whatsoever. While she sleeps, he watches over her. He sinks down next to her, slides over to her, and buries his nose in her hair. Her scent fills his head. Luna smells as sweet as a slice of cake. He slides a little closer, until he can feel the warmth of her tiny yet hefty body, and whispers, "Sweet pea," the way Mama sometimes does, and suddenly everything is right again, they're lying in a safe cocoon of warmth and fragrance. Henning thinks he hears his parents' voices off in the distance, like they're chitchatting in the main hall behind the house's thick walls, and he falls asleep.

He wakes with a start, as if someone had given him a shake or slapped his hands, and can't figure out where he is. The wall colors, the angle of the light, everything about the room is unfamiliar. At first he doesn't see Luna, who is still asleep, just the room's absolute disarray, like something has exploded. All he knows is that he's alone, in a strange place, and something awful has happened.

He jumps out of bed and heads toward the door; then he notices that it's Mama and Papa's things lying all over the floor, and his horror grows. The next moment he sees Luna asleep on the bed in her little dress, and his fear turns to relief: nap! Mama and Papa were gone, but they must have come back during naptime. Henning slept, too, which he hasn't done for a long time now, so he definitely has to tell Mama, she'll be surprised, she's always happy when the kids sleep and eat. They ate, too, Henning realizes, even if it was a little different than usual.

He has already run halfway down the corridor when it occurs to him that he can't leave Luna alone; if she wakes up and sees she's alone, she'll panic; so he goes to wake her. As he's shaking her shoulders with both hands, he sees that the bedcover underneath her is wet. She peed while she slept, right in the middle of Mama's bed. He hadn't put a diaper on her before naptime. A lump rises in Henning's throat, but he forces himself to swallow it, pull sleepy little Luna from the bed, and place a pillow over her pee-pee. They run off.

They search the entire house. Then the yard. Only afterward does the car pop back into Henning's mind. Right then, he takes a look. It's not there. Mama and Papa haven't come yet.

Time stands still. The day seems to dissolve in the heat. Time spreads out all around Henning like a surface upon which you could go in any direction at all and yet never arrive anywhere. Luna lies out on the terrace floor, her head resting on her arm like a pillow. Her free hand is playing with two little black stones, which she pushes back and forth, following the patterns on the floor tiles. It looks weird, Henning almost doesn't even recognize his sister like this. When he goes over and pokes her, she grunts, reluctant. Nothing is moving in the yard, not a single bird chirps, there isn't a breath of wind, even the palms have stopped rustling. Every now and then Henning goes to the driveway and looks down into the valley. He sees cars driving on the winding ribbon of road down below, but none are coming up toward them.

On his way to the kitchen, where he hopes

to find something to drink, Henning discovers more puddles and a little poop Luna has left in the main hall. His head empty, he stares at it for a long while, until his body starts moving again, taking him toward the bathroom to get more wet wipes. He lays a wet wipe over every smudge, that way the room looks better, like a bunch of white birds have flown in and landed all over, their wings spread out.

There's no juice left. In the fridge he finds another half container of milk. He drinks some, and brings the rest to Luna, but she doesn't get up, she just shakes her head, still lying down. He sets the container in front of her and waits. When his thirst overpowers him at some point, he drinks the rest himself. Now that they're out of both juice and milk, Papa and Mama really need to come back.

And they do come. The silence shifts, grows thicker somehow, and even Luna finally raises her head. They can hear a rumble, it grows louder and louder, it isn't a plane, it's a car.

"Caaar?" says Luna.

"It's them!" shouts Henning.

"Mamaaa!" Luna yells as she runs across the terrace to the steps, "Mamaaa!" as if Mama could hear her already, and maybe she really can. When they get to the driveway they see the car, it's still a ways away, slowly rumbling up the dirt road, the hood rises and falls, and here and there Henning hears the wheels spinning on the gravel, somehow it's an exciting noise. The car looks similar to their rental car, but it's a different color. Blue instead of white. It doesn't seem to bother Luna, she jumps for joy, calling "Mama, Mama, Mama," and waving her arms up in the air. And then Henning catches on: the other car broke down! They must have gotten a flat and had to get another car, that's why it took so long! Now he jumps and waves, too, calling out, "Hello, hello!" and he's happier than ever. For just a second the utter chaos inside comes to mind, but he immediately pushes the thought away.

The car's windshield flashes like a mirror in the direct sun. Henning and Luna step to one side as the car rolls up the driveway to the parking spot. Now you can see through the windshield, but Henning doesn't understand what he sees. There are four people in the car, two kids in the back seat, who wave and smile back at them, and up front a man behind the wheel and a woman in the passenger seat. They all have black hair. The man leans out his open window and says something that sounds like a question. Henning and Luna take a step back. The man repeats his question, he looks friendly, smiles, and says something else, then shakes his head and talks to his wife, who's holding a map in her lap. Henning and Luna stare at them, they don't understand a single word. The man says something else, laughs, points to the house and gives them a thumbs-up, as if to say, "Nice house!" and then turns the wheel and puts the car in reverse, he's turning around, Henning takes Luna by the hand and pulls her out of the way. The kids wave to them from the back seat. The car drives back down the mountain. Henning and Luna watch as it gets smaller and smaller until, far, far down, it turns off the dirt road and disappears between the little toy houses of the little toy village. It's completely quiet.

"That wasn't Mama and Papa," Henning says. "But they'll come soon, too."

As Henning says it, he has the awful feeling he's lying. The thought occurs to him that nobody will come. The island only had one car to send up to them, and it sent the wrong one. That's it.

He considers whether Mama and Papa might be dead. Henning knows all about death; he knows a lot about dinosaurs, how they went extinct, and why. He's already seen a lot of dead animals. Just a couple of days ago they found a bunny-rabbit skeleton in the yard, bright white, bleached by the sun, with eye sockets and teeth and all four legs. Henning got as excited as a treasure hunter, it was a valuable find, so he carefully picked up the bones and brought them to Papa, and Papa told him what all of them were called, skull, ribs, spine.

And because he's such a specialist, Henning knows that death is something for dinosaurs, lizards flattened by car tires, and birds who have flown into a windowpane so that they fall down and lie on their backs with their spindly legs sticking up in the air.

But not for parents. There is no such thing as dead parents. Parents have to take care of their kids, they can't just die. Maybe Mama and Papa had to go back to Germany all of a sudden, or they went to find some other kids because Luna can be super annoying and Henning still isn't fully able to do a lot of things he really should be able to. But they definitely haven't died.

Luna's crying, not out of rage, but softly. She goes over to Henning like a good little girl, and takes his hand, crying, and Henning realizes he has no idea what to do next. This not-knowing is the biggest thing he's ever had to face, bigger than the mountains, the sun, and the entire sky, it's a black nothingness as big as the universe itself.

The day spreads out stubbornly before them. It's impossible to play. They hang around on the terrace, and Henning notices how the color of the light begins to shift. He runs to their parents' bedroom just once, to check Papa's alarm clock and see whether the hands are still moving. He's relieved to see the skinny red hand turning in circles as usual.

When Luna starts her Mama-Mama whining again, Henning yells at her to stop. In the kitchen he pushes a chair into the pantry and climbs up to reach the shelf with another container of orange juice on it. He gets it down but can't get the cap off. He tries with all his might, until his fingers hurt, and then howls with rage. Then he gets a pair of scissors from the drawer. Scissors are off limits, too, but meanwhile Henning has almost stopped caring. He takes the scissors and stabs at the orange juice as if he were trying to slaughter an animal. Finally a slit appears and yellow liquid flows out. Henning presses his lips to it and sucks, but because the opening is fairly big and he's also wrestling with Luna, who's really thirsty, a lot of it gushes to the floor. They kneel on the tiles like animals, Luna's shrill shrieking fills the room. The container spills, and they lick the juice up off the floor. Henning doesn't even try to wipe up the rest. The house already looks like a battlefield anyway, the orange juice won't make any difference. Henning has even stopped bothering to put wet wipes over Luna's puddles. Once he stepped on a little pile of her poop and slipped, leaving brown skid marks on the floor. He took his socks off and washed his feet in the toilet. He didn't care. He hardly even notices the stench anymore, either.

What's most horrifying, though, is that Henning doesn't know when it's time to go to bed. He looks at Papa's alarm clock again. He knows the numbers, and he knows it's about seeing which hand points where, and that they're normally put to bed at eight o'clock. But the alarm clock doesn't want anything to do with it. One hand points to the nine, another to the four, and the little red hand evenly turns in its circle. In the summertime it's still light out when bedtime comes, so the sun is no help either. When Henning imagines nighttime surprising them out here on the terrace, a cold fear overcomes him. Maybe the monster comes out of the water tank at night and lurks around the terrace. Mama and Papa always insist that he and Luna go to bed right on time. He has to make sure they do. But is the right time now, this second, or the next one? He doesn't feel tired, and Luna hasn't yawned even once, either. She's sitting on the floor and playing with the little stones and seems perfectly content. When Henning looks at her, he's not sure what he feels. He's happy she's there. At the same time, he hates her, because she cries so much and knows so little and absolutely anything could happen to her at any moment.

Just when he can't stand the uncertainty any longer, he claps his hands twice and calls out, "And now it's bedtime!"

To his great surprise, Luna heaves herself up and runs off ahead of him into the bathroom, as if she'd been waiting for him to say "bedtime." He climbs up on the stool, gets the toothbrushes from the cup, twists the cap off the tube, and squeezes the toothpaste out, way too much but it doesn't matter, he smears the extra into the sink. Luna begins brushing her teeth without any resistance; when Mama's there, there's always a lot more drama. Henning heaps as much praise on her as he can, "Good job, Luna, you're doing great, such a good girl," then takes her toothbrush and even remembers to rinse it off. Luna sticks her arms up over her head so he can take her dress off. When she's naked, he sees how filthy she is. He'd like to just put a big towel over her, but he keeps chatting, "Lookie, that's no good, we need to clean you up a bit," and Luna lies down on the floor, the way she does on good days when Mama changes her diaper, and lets him clean her legs with the wet wipes. Most of the gunk has dried already, but Henning doesn't give up, he scrubs and rubs until Luna's skin is all red. He looks around and finds their pajamas and helps Luna put hers on, "You got it, now arms up again, watch your head," and as everything's going so well a wave of great relief sweeps through him. He was so afraid of going to bed, but it turns out to be no problem at all. Soon after that Luna is lying under the covers in their pushed-together bed and looks like she always does when it's time to go to sleep. She even says, "Storyyy?" like always. Henning runs back through the house looking for the book. The sun is still up, just like when they went to bed yesterday and the day before, and the color of light Henning sees in the windows is exactly right. Next to the couch in the main hall he finds *Pony, Bear and Apple Tree*, their favorite book, which Mama has read to them so many times that Henning knows every sentence by heart. He sits next to Luna in bed, she cuddles up next to him, and he makes like he's reading to her, pointing to the pictures and reciting the words. "This is a tree. A tree and a tree and yet another tree are a forest." Luna gets excited about all the words she knows. "In the forest there is a clearing, in the clearing there is a house, behind the house there is an apple tree." Luna points to the pictures and says, "tree," "house," and "apple." "Once upon a time, there lived a pony," says Henning. He reads the whole book. He reads it once again, after Luna has already fallen asleep. Then he says to himself, aloud, "Now, that's enough. Time to go to sleep," he puts the book down on the floor and slips under the thin covers. He slides over, close to Luna, and sticks his nose into her hair.

But then it happens. The house starts to transform. The corridors grow longer, the walls thicker. The rooms change places. The roof sinks low, as if trying to squish the kids, then it soars up again into the sky. The masonry moans and groans, the lamp turns into the beak of a huge bird about to peck at Henning. Now he knows he wasn't afraid of going to bed, he was afraid of being in bed. They've never been all alone at night, Mama and Papa were always there, and they made sure the house didn't play such wild tricks and that no monsters came in. Henning mustn't think about the monster or he'll be sick. He mustn't think about how the rectangular hole in the floor looks, the hole they peered down into, right there, just outside the house, in complete darkness, with the mirror-like blackness at the bottom. Now he understands why the woman on the wall is crying red tears. She knew from the very start what was going to happen.

The room grows ever darker. Henning knows that; he's often watched the darkness come, when he couldn't sleep. Shadows grow in the corners. Everything has a different face. Henning's eyes hurt under the strain, he's shutting them so tight. With all his might, he tries not to think about the monster. Normally, right about now he'd run to

Mama and say, "My brain is trembling," and she'd take him into her arms as he cried a little and he would sniff her and play with her hair and she'd say "Shh-shh," even though she would be annoyed because she actually wanted her peace and quiet at night.

But Mama is gone, so his brain can tremble all it wants. Could it tremble so hard that his head will burst open? Above all he mustn't look at Luna. She's lying right by his side, sleeping with her mouth open and snoring a little bit, but if he looks at her even a tiny bit longer her sweet, peaceful little face transforms into a terrifying, grotesque grimace with torn-open jaws and spiky teeth, and Henning slams his eyes shut, his heart is beating like a drum, and the woman on the wall isn't looking up above anymore, but directly at him, staring straight into his soul.

Henning thinks Mama and Papa are gone because he stepped on the cracks between the tiles. Sometimes he played "Step on a crack, break your mama's back" on the terrace, telling himself, "If I can't get to the other side without stepping on a crack, something really terrible will happen." But he was just playing. It was just a game. He thought. But then he ran across the terrace so many times not paying any attention, and just think how many cracks he must have stepped on!

He feels like crying, but even his tears are afraid, so they don't even dare to leave his eyes.

When he wakes up, he immediately knows where he is and what's happened. He knows his location and situation down to the smallest detail. Today he won't run through the house looking for Mama and Papa. They're gone, they're not coming back, and somehow it's Henning's fault. He discovers both stones in his fists, scarab and millipede, he must have grabbed them from the bedposts before falling asleep, and not let go the entire night.

When he gets up he sees that Luna has wet the bed. Her pajamas have a dark spot on them, and the sheet underneath her has a big stain. A frightening anger rises within him. Where will they sleep when all the beds have been peed in? Henning can't change the sheets on a whole bed, no way, he can't! And at some point she'll poop in bed, and then? What happens then?

He shakes her arm so hard that she wakes up with a scream.

"You peed!" he yells. "That's bad! Bad!"

Luna looks at him, uncomprehending, her big eyes heavy with sleep. He grabs her by the shoulders and turns her so she has to look at the stain.

"There! Pee-pee! Bad!"

"Pee-peee? Luna pee-peee?"

Her face twists into a grimace and she starts bitterly crying. Henning's anger grows.

"Crying won't help anything!" he shouts. "Crying won't make the pee-pee go away!"

He wants to cover the stain, maybe with a hand towel. Since Luna's still sitting on it, he yanks her arm to pull her down from the bed. She doesn't put up a fight, she just collapses in on herself and cries. Using both hands, he shoves her toward the edge of the bed.

"Bad! Pee-pee bad!"

One last push, and she tumbles out of bed.

The sound she makes as she hits the floor is terrifying. A flat plop, followed immediately by a dull thud, which thumps right through Henning's entire body. That was her head. Worse than that sound is the silence that follows. Like every morning, the birds out in the yard are quite loud. The raspy call of the red-backed shrike sitting on the edge of the outer garden wall, a lizard in its beak, about to feed its chicks. The hoopoe's *whoop-hoop-hoop*. The sparrows' lively chirping as they nest in the palms. High above, circling seagulls, whose calls are carried on the wind. Mama told them about all the birds, and she's thrilled when the kids show an interest in them. But what use is his knowledge of birds? None at all. It's superfluous, useless. Above all, when you know things, it just makes everything worse.

Henning knows you can die if you fall out of bed. Especially if your head hits the floor hard. Mama has explained it to him a million times. He mustn't push Luna, especially not in bed or on the stairs. He knows her head could break open and then everything comes out and Luna's dead.

She starts screaming. The silence explodes, her roar is deafening. But Henning doesn't feel relieved, he just feels even more furious. He runs to the bathroom to look for a towel, and as he searches he hurls everything from the cabinets, Mama's brushes, rolls of toilet paper, bars of soap, he runs back with the hand towel, covers the stain on the bed, and takes a deep breath. Without even glancing at Luna as she lies shrieking on the floor, he leaves the room, goes to pee, and then goes to the kitchen. He's hungry. Horribly hungry.

It doesn't take long for her to follow him, her face streaked with tears, her little body still shaking, her sobs ebbing. He can't bear to look at her, especially the bump on her forehead. Reaching her little arms out toward him, she shuffles over for a hug, but he pushes her away.

"Go away. You stink."

In the pantry he discovers a jar with little sausages in it, up high, so Luna and Henning can't get to it. He pushes a chair over, sets an upside-down pot on top of it, and climbs up. The whole thing wobbles, especially when he gets up on his tippy-toes and stretches his arms up.

"Move to the side!" he calls to Luna, who's watching him, wide-eyed. He slides the jar off the shelf, it crashes onto the tiles and rolls aside, but doesn't break.

"Dammit," Henning shouts, and Luna laughs. Henning feels a desire to laugh, too, in his belly. They're not supposed to say "dammit," Papa freaks out when they do, but sometimes they do it anyway, whispering in bed, laughing so hard they almost die. But now he's got to get the jar open. He needs ideas. He imagines he's an architect. They always have good ideas. He climbs onto the table, raises the jar high above his head, gathers all his strength, and throws it full-force onto the floor. It shatters, the liquid splashes all the way to the walls, the shards clink across the floor. Luna has already devoured the first little sausage before Henning can even clamber down from the table. She shoves it halfway into her mouth, almost gags, and puts all her effort into chewing. Henning takes two little sausages in each hand, and when Luna sees that she grabs another, swipes a third one, and runs from the room like a little animal carrying booty back to its stash. Henning stuffs it all down until he can't anymore, still kneeling on the floor, almost four sausages already. One of the glass shards is still full of liquid, and Henning carefully raises it to his lips and drinks it all down.

When he goes to look for Luna, she's not in the main hall. He spots the nubby end of a sausage on the tiles, but no trace of her. Henning runs to their parents' bedroom and opens the door just a crack. The chaos is still there, but Luna isn't. He finally finds her in the bathroom, in front of the toilet. She's lifted the lid and seat, and has stuck one of her arms down into the bowl. Cupping her fingers, she tries to scoop up some water, dipping her hand in and licking it.

"No!" yells Henning. "Don't drink from the toilet!"

He wraps his arms around her midriff and pulls her away, she doesn't wail, stays quiet as a mouse, but doggedly squirms. He still manages to drag her out of the bathroom and push her to the floor.

"Poison! Mama says so! Water bad!"

"Wadda baaad?"

"There's monster pee in there! We can only drink the water from the canisters."

"Monstaaa?"

"Yup. Monster-water. Don't drink from the toilet. Bad."

As Luna calms down, he lets her sit up. For the first time today he really looks at her face. Her eyes are red, and there's a dried-up, whitish coating on her lips. And the awful bump. Luna looks sick, like on the days Mama puts her hand on her forehead and gives her a suppository at night. Henning doesn't know how much water she drank out of the toilet. He desperately hopes she doesn't die. He promises he'll be nicer to her.

Of course he's thirsty, too. Deeply thirsty, outrageously thirsty, it feels like there's a little spiny-skinned animal in his throat. And there's no milk. Henning can't get to the canisters, they're too heavy, he can't open them, and their plastic is so thick the scissors just slide right off. He doesn't know where they can get any water. There's the garden hose out in the yard, which Noah uses to water the bushes, but Henning has no idea if he'd be able to turn it on, and doesn't even know whether you're supposed to drink from it, either.

"C'mon, sweet pea," he says to Luna, in the tone Mama uses. "We've got a plan."

Now Henning knows what they'll do. He's made a decision. They'll go to Femés to look for Mama and Papa. Maybe they just couldn't find the dirt road leading back up the mountain, and they're still wandering around town. When Mama drives him to nursery school, she always lets him give her directions, turn left here, go straight, then turn right up there. He never gets lost.

"If I didn't have you," Mama then says, "I'd never find my way home." Mama needs his help, he'll track her down and show her the way. On the way to the terrace, Luna holds his hand like a good girl.

"We need shoes," says Henning.

He's thought of everything. You can't walk on the dirt road with your bare feet, or even in stocking feet. Since he failed with Luna's sneakers, he'll try with her slippers, the ones with the hard soles. They have Velcro, so he should be able to do it.

Indeed, it's no problem at all. Luna sits

down on the floor and sticks her feet out toward him, he slips them on her and closes the Velcro straps.

"We're going to look for Mama. In Femés."

"Feméééés?"

"Into the village. We're going to pick her up."

As Henning puts his own shoes on, Luna stomps impatiently and laughs. When she starts running out ahead of him, Henning shouts "Hand!" and she stays put until he takes her by the hand.

They cross the terrace and go down the steps nice and slow. As Luna is about to step onto the gravel with her front foot, she stops.

"What's wrong?"

"Fwip-per."

He doesn't know what she means, and tries to pull her forward, but she's locked in place. Then he realizes, she has her slippers on, and you're really not supposed to go outside in your slippers.

"It's okay," he says. "This is an exception."

She lets him lead her off the last step, but then she wants to take her shoes off again.

"No!" Henning shouts. "Leave them on.

You need shoes. C'mon! Let's go get Mama!"

Instead of walking along with him, she swats at his hand, chases him, lets out an angry grunt.

"Are you nuts?" Henning swats back, now she's really wailing. Being nice doesn't work, but it's not his fault. Luna's acting like a baby, but she's already two. She sits on the bottom step and sulks. He grabs her upper arms and shakes her as hard as he can.

"Y'know what I'm gonna do? If you don't come with, I'll take you to the spiders! I'll shove you against the wall and the spiders will crawl all over you, your whole body, even your face!"

"No pider," Luna howls. "No pider!"

"C'mon then. Otherwise, spiders!"

Finally she stands up and gets moving. As they start down the driveway, Henning realizes they still have their pajamas on. He forgot to get dressed, and to dress Luna. Shame lands on the nape of his neck but then flies away again, like an insect that's decided to go bite someone else.

As soon as they set foot on the dirt road it gets super steep. Luna starts slipping, he holds her arm with both hands and makes sure she doesn't fall. They've never walked this part, only driven it, in the car. but Henning knows they'll make it—after all, they can already see Femés. He can hear the hammering and the barking dogs. What he doesn't like, though, is how the mountains across the valley are looking over at them. Their sheer silence seems to jeer at him and Luna.

But he has no time to think about that. They have to concentrate on walking. The ground is covered in gravel and dirt, and their shoes can't get enough traction. Some of the potholes are so deep it's better to walk around them. To the right and left of the road, rabbits dart in and out of the thorn bushes, and Luna yelps with excitement when she sees one. She keeps falling on her bum, Henning can't prevent that. Even he falls at one point, but he gets right back up again, even though he's scraped his knuckles.

He imagines he's an architect and Luna is his assistant. They're climbing around a construction site where a huge house is going to be built. Down below, the builders are waiting for Henning's instructions. He hears them hammering, but unless he gets there really soon, they won't be able to keep building. The route there is difficult and stressful, but it's completely clear that the architect and his assistant will make it. They're strong people, for whom a dirt road poses no real problem.

The sun burns bright. Henning knows he should have thought to get their sun hats. But he didn't, and he's too exhausted to get angry over it. There isn't any shade on the entire mountainside, no trees, no palms, no walls, just squat thornbushes and rocks. Up in the sky the sun turns everything around itself white, like it's burning through the blue sky. Henning always thought of the sun as his friend. Now he's not so sure anymore. Sweat burns his eyes, he can't stop blinking because his vision is growing blurry. Luna staggers. She's falling more than walking. Lurching. And she's very quiet. She no longer yelps at the rabbits, and doesn't even really seem to notice where she is. His hands are hurting from trying to hold on to her, and his head hurts, as much as his feet and his knuckles do where he tripped and got scraped up.

On the first curve he decides to take a break. He looks down into the valley, trying to judge the distance, and is startled. The village isn't any closer, it's actually slid farther away. Like if you were looking at it through binoculars turned the wrong way. The dirt road below them snakes onward, endless. Henning can't even count all the curves. His head hurts so much that he can barely even see.

In the car it was always so fast. The panorama bobbed up and down outside the windows, and sometimes Papa pretended they were playing Paris–Dakar Rally, bending far over the steering wheel and letting Mama give him directions, "Hard right," "Left, make a U-turn." Henning and Luna bounced and cheered in the back seat. But now they're sticking to the ground like flies whose wings have been torn off.

We aren't architects, Henning thinks, we're just little kids.

Despite the fact that he's crying, no tears

come, even though his whole body is shaking. His face is dry as a bone. He's sat down on the ground and dropped his head into his hands. He sits like that until the shaking stops. As he looks up again, and gazes toward town, he sees the car. A white Opel, smaller than a toy car. It's driving slowly down one of the lanes, stops at a traffic light, turns its blinker on. Even from way up here Henning sees it. The car turns and disappears among the houses. The rental car. That's their rental car! It's exactly like he thought. Mama and Papa are wandering around down there, lost.

"Luna! They're down there! I saw them!"

Luna has lain down on her tummy, right there on the dirt road, even though it must hurt. She doesn't respond. Only when he shakes her shoulder does she lift her head a little.

"I saw Mama and Papa! We gotta keep going!"

Luna's head sinks back down. Henning stands up, tries to pull her to her feet. She's softly grumbling, reluctant.

"Look, over there, goats!"

It's true, on one of the slopes opposite you

can see a bunch of colorful dots, a whole herd, some with spots, some all white. Henning can even make out the herdsman and his dog, before it all blurs up and he has to blink again. Luna loves goats. Whenever Mama spots a goat, Luna is the first to run over and see.

"Tired," Luna says, so quietly he can barely understand her. Henning gives up.

"Well you can just stay here, then. I'll go without you. Bye!"

Sometimes Mama does this when Luna refuses to budge. She walks off, and pretends she's going to leave, just letting Luna sit and pout, defiant, arms crossed tight over her chest. Usually it works. At some point Luna just can't stand it anymore, and jumps up, running after her. Only on really bad days does Mama have to turn around, pick Luna up, screaming and kicking, and carry her in her arms.

Henning walks away. His legs are rusty for the first few steps, but then it goes better.

"I'm really going, Luna! Bye-bye!"

Every few steps he turns his head back. Luna doesn't look at him even once. He doesn't even know if she's caught on that he's going ahead.

Then Henning has an idea. He really will leave her here. He'll run into town by himself, as fast as he can, because with her he'll never make it. He'll find Mama and Papa, get into the car with them, and they'll drive back here and pick up Luna. And there's always a bottle of water in the car, that's what makes him happiest right now, just thinking about it.

He goes back to Luna to explain the plan.

"You wait here, okay? I'll be right back. I'm getting Mama and Papa."

At first she seems not to react even to that, but then she lifts her head and looks at him. Her eyes are even redder, her hair drenched with sweat, and the white coating now goes from her lips up over her nose.

"Don' go," she says.

"Real quick. To get Mama and Papa. Right back."

"Don' go!"

He bends over and kisses her on the head. Then he walks off. She starts crying. He goes as far as he can, as fast as he can. He doesn't want to turn around, but does anyway. She's struggled up partway, is kneeling on the dirt road, stretching her arms out toward him, trying to get up and continually falling back down.

"Henni! Henni! Henni!"

She isn't calling for Mama, she's calling for him. Every time she calls his name, it cuts into him like a knife. He keeps going, doesn't turn around, doesn't hear her anymore, doesn't see her anymore, falls, stands back up, keeps going.

At the next curve he takes a break. He looks into the valley. The rental car has vanished; Henning sees a blue car and a red car, but no white car. The white one must be driving in circles around the toy lanes, hidden behind the toy houses. It shouldn't be hard to find their car, Femés isn't so big. But it has slid a little farther into the distance again. No matter how much Henning blinks or squints, it doesn't look any closer. He has to hurry up and get there, or else eventually it will be entirely gone. Maybe he should run, even if that does increase the danger of falling.

He turns around and looks back. Up above, on the side of the road, Luna is lying face-down. She isn't moving. You can't see her head, just the baby-blue fabric of her pajamas, which were hand-me-downs from him.

She looks like roadkill. A cat. A bunny rabbit. One of those animals just lying on the road, drying up in the sun, that will get flatter and flatter as more cars drive over them, until they're smashed to bits, their fur falls off, their guts go all over the road, and then one day when you drive by all you see are some brownish stains on the asphalt.

Henning's legs start running before he has even told them to. Not downhill, but uphill. They turn away from Femés, and run back up the dirt road. Back to Luna.

As they lie next to one another on the cool terrace, Henning can hardly believe they made it back to the house. He carried and dragged Luna farther than she actually walked. He yelled at her and implored her, promised her rewards, threatened her, pulled at her arms and legs, pushed and shoved her. Despite all that, she still only managed to stay on her feet for a couple of steps before falling right back down again. He sat down right next to her and as the sun beat down he waited for his strength to return. The entire time the house remained in view, right before his eyes, beaming white from behind the walls and palms, not so far away and yet utterly unreachable. He thought they'd never make it. Nevertheless, he just kept going.

The shade is like an embrace, cool, with a slightly floral scent, like when Mama comes out of the bathroom freshly showered and lays her hands lightly on Henning's shoulders. He turns his head, to alternate which cheek is touching the cool tiles. His skin burns, and a throbbing pain feels like it's going to make his skull explode. But the worst is the spiny animal in his throat. When Henning tries to swallow, he chokes. Next to him, Luna looks like she's asleep, her eyes are closed and she's breathing softly. Rest a little, thinks Henning, and then we'll try a second time. Maybe he can take the baby buggy, to push Luna. Or the wheelbarrow, like Noah did. That was always so fun, riding around the yard with Noah! Noah, who stole Mama and killed Papa. But they aren't dead, because parents don't die, they're just driving around Femés in the white Opel, lost. Behind his closed eyelids Henning sees the pattern of the cracks on the tile floor, the cracks he shouldn't have stepped on. Then he falls asleep.

When he wakes up, it seems like no time at all has passed. The yard is as quiet as before, motionless in the heat. Luna's eyes are closed, she's lying on the floor, and hasn't moved. Henning can't tell whether it's morning or afternoon, he's stuck in the day, time has turned into a trap. But he does feel a little stronger, his headache is a little bit better and his eyes don't burn as much as before. He pushes himself up and goes into the kitchen, he needs something to quiet his upset stomach.

Kneeling in front of the fridge, he reaches all the way to the back and pulls out a big yogurt container. Henning doesn't even like yogurt, the sour taste reminds him of puke, and the yogurt here on the island has an extra strange goat-like smell; but Mama says over and over that there's nothing healthier in the entire world. He twists the top off, Mama would be proud of him, she'd smile and softly say, "See?" On top of the white stuff there's a layer of cloudy liquid, Henning drinks and can't help but close his eyes, the wetness makes his sore throat feel so good. He takes his fingers and shovels the yogurt down. The spiny animal loosens its claws, the yogurt pushes it down his throat and it disappears into his tummy. Henning has never tasted anything so delicious.

Before the container is completely empty, he remembers he should give some to Luna. He even remembers to bring a spoon, so she can reach the rest of it more easily. Out on the terrace he stops in his tracks, closes and opens his eyes over and over, because he can't believe what he sees: nothing. Luna is gone. The spot where she had been, empty. Henning runs back and forth on the terrace, as if he might've overlooked her. But he already knows where she is. She's where Mama and Papa are. But how's that possible? Did Noah come, in secret, while Henning was in the kitchen? There's another possibility, more horrifying than anything else he's thought of so far. Henning refuses to even think it. Instead he runs through the house, through the main hall and all the corridors, and yells her name, hysterically, panicked, in a voice he doesn't even recognize.

"Luna!"

He finds her in the bathroom. She's managed to push the little cabinet closer to the sink, and has climbed up on it. Mama's jars of cream are on the floor, along with the half-empty package of wet wipes and a stack of facecloths. Plus the toothbrushes and toothpaste. The faucet is running. Luna is holding the cup that had held the toothbrushes under the stream of water. She fills it up, and drinks. When she spots Henning, she drinks faster. She gulps, trying to empty it one more time. The eyes he sees peering back at him from over the rim of the cup are unnaturally large, like the eyes of a nocturnal animal.

Henning's horror turns into hate. He hates Luna, hates her with all his might. Because she absolutely knows she's not supposed to do that. Because she never does as she's told. Because she gave him such a shock by suddenly disappearing. Because she's drinking water that will kill her. Because Mama and Papa will say he didn't take good care of her. Because in his hand he's holding a container with a few sad bits of yogurt he wanted to give her. Because the spiny animal is back in his throat now. Because he himself needs water too, an entire tubful, so he can dive in, drink, drink, and cool his body off both inside and out.

"Waddaaa," Luna says, briefly setting the cup down so she can catch her breath.

He shoves her. Away from the poisonous water, away from the sink.

"Bad!"

The cup flies through the air. The little cabinet topples. Luna falls with her hands out, trying to catch herself, and actually does land on her arms, but the momentum is too strong, she can't break her fall, and her chin hits the colorful tile floor. This time Henning knows she's not dead, because she didn't land on the back of her head, she landed on her face. But something else happens, maybe actually worse than dying. Within seconds everything is covered in blood. Henning has never seen so much blood. It's coming from Luna, running over her cheeks and into her ears, and then changes direction as she sits up, over her chin and throat and onto her baby-blue pajama top, which quickly turns dark red. Luna is so bewildered that she doesn't even scream. She touches her face and looks at her red hands. She quizzically looks at Henning, as if he needs to explain something to her. As she opens her mouth to say something, still more blood comes out, an entire torrent. Luna coughs, blood spatters onto his pajama bottoms, his arms, and his face.

He made all this blood come out. He shoved her. It's his fault.

"Stop bleeding," he growls at her. "Quit it, now!"

Luna looks terrified, she doesn't understand what he's saying, but she can tell from his tone how furious he is.

"Only because of you! Because you drank the monster-water! It's all your fault."

Only now does she start crying, and not because she's bleeding, but because he's scolding her, and that makes Henning even more furious. As she cries her mouth twists, her lips part, blood and spittle fly out, and Henning can see what has happened. She's missing two front teeth. The top two. Where they used to be is now a bloody, rectangular hole. Henning knows you can't just put teeth back in again. Everybody will see that they're missing. He feels the urge to shove Luna again, so hard that she flies across the bathroom, maybe hitting her head on the toilet, and then she'll just lie there and be quiet, and finally he'll have some peace.

"I'm going now," he says. "I'll only come back if you stop bleeding!"

He runs through the main hall and hides behind the couch. The colorful cover is hanging down, and he pulls it over himself so Luna won't be able to find him. He hears her crying, hears her coming closer, "Henni! Henni! Henni!" He holds his breath, sits tight, and forces himself to just stay put until she finally falls silent.

Just as it's getting dark, he brings Luna to bed. This time he didn't manage to beat the darkness, but he's too tired to even worry about that. He found the two teeth in the bathroom and picked them out of the pool of dried blood. As he's placing them under her pillow, he tells Luna the story of the tooth fairy. Luna is lying on her back and staring straight into his eyes the entire time. As if she wanted to drink his gaze up. There are still some black flakes of dried blood around her mouth and on her throat, he didn't manage to get them all off. But he put her in clean pajamas, an effort Henning is very proud of. He gently pats her on the head and says, "Oh, Luna," until she closes her eyes. Sleep is a magnificent realm, and Henning runs toward it with speedy steps. Sleep surrounds him, embraces him, obliterates everything else. Henning plunges into forgetting.

When he wakes up, he knows the answer. It's right in front of his eyes, crystal clear, as if he'd known the entire time. Maybe he just didn't want to believe it. Refused to accept it. Henning gets up, goes to the bathroom, pees in the toilet, goes back to the main hall, and finds Luna. He hadn't even noticed that she wasn't next to him when he woke up. She's acting a little strange, cowering against a wall, hugging her knees to her chest with her arms, and rocking forwards and backwards. Once, at the zoo, Henning saw a monkey sitting behind a big glass windowpane and acting like this. Once again her eyes look unnaturally large as she gazes back at him. She doesn't say a word, doesn't react to his presence in any way, just keeps rocking and watching. Henning wonders whether she's drunk more water in secret. But it doesn't matter now. He needs her. He has a plan, but he needs her help with it, he can't do it on his own.

"C'mon," he says. "I know what happened."

The sun shines bright and fills the main hall with a friendly glow. Out on the terrace it's already quite warm. Up in the palms, the sparrows are making a major ruckus. Henning and Luna exit the terrace and walk all the way around the house. The spider wall is covered in spiders, hundreds of them, spine-chilling eight-legged suns, utterly motionless. The mere sight of them makes Henning feel as if they're already all over his body. Hand in hand, they run right past. Luna feels hot to the touch. Her entire body is emanating heat, like she's burning from within. When she realizes where they're headed, she stops in her tracks.

"Yeah, I know," Henning says. "But this has to be it."

They're standing at the edge of the cement surface, the spot that Papa explained collects rainwater into the aljibe. Before, there was only rainwater for people, animals, and plants, and since it so rarely rains here on the island, every single drop has to be captured and saved. Luna stamps her foot on the floor and stares out over the heavy board that Papa put over the hole in the middle of the area so that nobody could fall in. She hasn't forgotten what Mama said: "A monster lives down there. If you get too close, it'll pull you in."

And then that's what happened to Mama. Henning knew the whole time, he just didn't have the courage to admit it. Because he knows exactly what monsters are like, he knows about them from countless stories. Mama was working out in the yard and just wanted to see if there was still water in the aljibe. The very moment she lifted the board up, a hand on a long arm shot up and pulled her in. Maybe Papa heard her scream and tried to help, and so the monster pulled him in, too.

Henning can't figure out what happened with the car. But right now it doesn't strike him as very important. What's important is that Mama and Papa are sitting down there in the water, in the dark, guarded by a monster sneering at them with his hideous face. Maybe the monster has already eaten one of them, but Henning can't even think past that point.

Luna shakes her head. Her eyes have grown even larger. Her whole face looks like it consists solely of two huge eyes.

"Mama and Papa are down there," Henning says. "We have to bring them back up."

"Mamaaa? Papaaa?"

Henning realizes he's hearing Luna's voice for the first time in a long while. He lets out a laugh, even though he really isn't in the mood to laugh. He kneels down to hug his sister. She presses her burning little body against him. She lays her head on his shoulder, and breathes like she's about to fall asleep.

"C'mon. We can rest later. Let's get Mama and Papa out of the hole."

They cross the concrete surface with small,

light steps, as if they were walking on thin ice. The closer they come to the hole, the slower their progress seems. Luna keeps stopping and shaking her head, then Henning takes her hand so she'll keep going. He can't stop talking, the words just keep tumbling from his lips. He tells her how one winter Papa took him to the reservoir. The water had frozen, and there was even a thin layer of snow on top. He and Papa went for a walk out on the lake. "You weren't with us, Luna," he says, "back then you were still really little." The water, Papa explained, always freezes from the edges in, so they stayed near the shore, since Papa couldn't be sure the ice in the middle would hold them. Suddenly they saw someone ice-skating in circles that went a little farther out. The skates drew a pretty pattern in the snow cover. The ice sang out and groaned, making strange noises Henning had never heard before. Then there was a muffled cracking sound, and the ice-skater vanished. Almost immediately he popped back up again, yelled, spat, and put his arms on the edge of the hole in the ice, trying to pull himself out. But the ice just kept breaking. The man thrashed about in the water, calling for help. Papa had already run off. He went to shore, and came back with a long branch. He laid down flat on his stomach and carefully crawled toward the hole in the ice. He stretched the end of the branch out to the skater, who grabbed on to it, and little by little, really slowly, Papa pulled him out of the hole. "He saved his life," Henning says.

Only when they get to the board do the words stop coming. They stand together and look at it. The board is bigger than Henning remembered. It looks like it was a door once, not a normal door for a house or a room, but maybe the door of a shed or stable. It's made of a bunch of different parts, all held together by slats nailed in at an angle. Henning kneels. The surface underneath his feet doesn't feel secure, like he's swaying slightly and could fall in at any moment. He feels the blackness beneath the concrete. He sticks his fingers under the edge of the board and tries to shake it. It barely moves. When he tries to lift it, nothing happens. Leaning slightly forward, he pushes up from his knees against the weight, heaves it with all his might, actually manages to lift it an inch or so, and when he lets go it falls right back into the same position as before. Its boom reverberates underground, with an echo that seems to encompass the whole yard. Like the monster's voice. Luna is transfixed with terror, her wide eyes look inquiringly at Henning.

"We can do it," Henning says. "Wait here."

He runs across the concrete, sure-footed this time, because he has a plan, he knows what to do. He'll get Mama and Papa out of there. Soon all four of them will sit in the white Opel again and wave at other kids standing by the side of the road. Out in the yard he finds a stone that will work. It's as big as a baby's head. He lifts it with both hands, holds it against his chest, and carries it over to the hole, where Luna is crouched on the concrete, waiting like a good little girl. He sets the stone down and is careful not to make a racket, so as not to scare her again. Although the sun burns hot and his headache is returning and he also forgot the sun hats again, he feels strong.

"Now you need to help," he says to Luna

using his architect voice. That's how he talks to her when they're building something together. Henning gives instructions, and Luna carries them out as best she can. He praises her a lot, because he knows that then she'll play with him longer.

"I'm the crane, you're the bulldozer. I'm going to lift this, and when it's high enough, you push the stone under there."

To be sure she's understood, he explains it a few more times in her language, "Bull-dozaaa, puuush!" and lets her try moving the stone a little. On the flat concrete, it's no problem. He gets into position and gives the signal.

"Ready, set, go."

This time he heaves from his knees to begin with, the board lifts up, and they're just a hand's width from being able to fit the stone under the edge. Henning's body is shaking, he's holding his breath, and he feels like all his blood is rushing to his head. The next few inches seem harder than the first ones, tougher, insurmountable. He thinks about Mama, how she's siting in the black water, and then he manages it.

"Now! Quick!" Luna pushes the stone, the board has fallen a little lower again, Henning heaves it back up with all his might, "Push!" the stone is in place and Henning can let go. His arms are rubber, he has to sit down. Sweat is burning his eyes, his mouth feels like sandpaper, but the lid is now nice and open. He lies down on the concrete and tries to see through the slit. It doesn't work, because he doesn't want to stick his head under the board, but he feels the cool air pouring out from below, it's cooling his forehead and feels really good.

"Hello!" he calls in. "Mama?"

The echo turns his voice into a strange being. It doesn't sound like it came from Henning's mouth, now it sounds like it's rising from below, along with the cool air. Luna lies down next to him and joins the chorus.

"Mamaaa! Mamaaa!"

They keep calling for a while, even though they don't get any answer. It feels good to yell, and the echo is even a little funny. At some point Henning says it's enough, and that they need to get back to work.

"Mama not theeere?"

"She's there. She's just not answering because she's … she's too weak. Or the monster is holding her mouth shut."

If Henning squats down low, he can get the balls of his thumbs under the edge of the board. That works much better than before, it lets him use a lot more force.

"Now you're a crane, too. Grab on. Get board up."

Luna stands next to him and wraps her fingers around the edge.

"Ready, set, go."

The board immediately rises. Henning pushes harder. It's got to come from your legs, Papa always says when he hoists something. Henning notices it's true. He manages to stand up, now the board is at his chest, which is pretty painful. Luna can only reach the edge by sticking her arms out. She's not really helping, she's just playing along.

"Go to the shorter side, there you'll be able to reach."

She gets it, and grabs on to the shorter side. Henning's feet are right on the edge of the hole. It occurs to him that he isn't wearing any shoes. His toes curl around the edge, like a monkey's when it's holding on to a tree. The movement pries a few pebbles loose and they fall into the hole. Henning hears them hit the water far below, making a hollow splash. The cold air blows against his legs and stomach, while the sun burns hot against his back. It's as if he were stuck between two seasons.

"We're almost there," he says to Luna, even though in reality he's not sure what's next. Even if he can get the board a little higher all by himself, it still won't be enough to get it to tip over. To reach the tipping point he'd have to take a couple of steps forward, but the hole is right there.

"Let's both grab the sides," he says. "Me here, you there."

He's not quite sure how this is supposed to go, but you simply have to try. Little by little he inches his way under the board, until he's standing across from Luna.

"When I say 'now,' we'll push as hard as we can."

Luna starts right then and there, pushing against the edge, as much as she can. Suddenly she slips.

"Careful!" Henning shouts.

A few larger pebbles plop down into the water below as Luna's legs dangle in the air, she holds onto the edge of the board but then falls, landing with her back on the concrete, her legs under the board. It looks like the hole is trying to swallow her up, suck her in, only her upper body is still visible. Henning can barely hold the board up by himself, but he can't let go, it would crush her.

There's a car. Henning doesn't hear it, and then he does.

"Crawl out! Quick!"

Luna has nowhere to put her legs down, and her fingers can't get a grip on the concrete surface, but she's a clever girl, she moves her body like a snake and makes progress one inch at a time.

The car comes closer, it doesn't sound like it's coming from Femés, it sounds like it's coming from the dirt road. Henning hears it and he doesn't hear it.

Little by little Luna gets away from the hole. Her feet are already brushing against the concrete, she's safe, she crawls forward on all fours.

"Well done! You're amazing!"

Henning's chest hurts from the weight of the board.

"And now push again!"

Luna stands up and grabs on to the edge again. A car door closes. Henning lifts his head and listens. It must have been his imagination. An echo hovering over the valley like a specter.

"Push!"

The board moves. It stands up straight. Henning takes a step forward.

"Hola? Hola!"

A man's voice. It has no place in this picture. It must have bounced off the silence of the yard. The board begins sliding. It slides diagonally over the hole, because Henning is pushing so much harder than Luna, and he can't hold it straight.

"No! Qué estáis haciendo? No!"

It's Noah. He's bounding across the yard. His mouth is gaping wide. Now Henning hears him shouting. The board slides and pushes Luna toward the hole, but she doesn't let go, she's already hanging halfway in.

"No!"

Noah is on the concrete. He's coming closer. Henning recognizes him. He knows who he is.

"Let go, Luna! Let go!"

She can't let go anymore, she needs the support. The board dips a little lower, Henning desperately fights to keep it balanced. Noah is coming closer. Henning sees his face, which has transformed into a hideous grimace. Then he gets it. The monster isn't in the hole. Noah is the monster. He pounced on Mama because he wanted to gobble her up. Then he came back and took both their parents. And now he wants the kids.

Henning starts screaming. The scream fills his head and chest. He can't hold the board anymore, it slips from his fingers. Noah has just grabbed Luna with one arm, and he's wrapping the other around Henning's hips. Henning thrashes, wriggles, screams, the board falls, crashing down with a deafening thud. Luna's screaming, too. The monster is holding them both tight. Henning struggles and already knows he has lost. He gave it his all, did everything he could, and still lost. This is the end.

HE STANDS AT the edge of the hole and stares into the void. The tipped-over board lies on the concrete nearby. Cool air wafts up into his face from below, the sun high in the sky burns the nape of his neck. Underneath, the water's surface is smooth as black glass, except for the occasional ripple, as if the mountain were trembling within.

"What's going on?"

Henning is winded, as if he'd been running. He notices he's holding something, opens his fists, and sees two painted stones, one in each hand, millipede on the left, scarab on the right. In a fit of fright, he hurls them away like something repugnant. They plunge into the hole, hit the water, their hollow-sounding splash sparks an echo, and concentric circles rupture the darkness for a

few brief moments, until silence and still-
ness regain the upper hand.

"Are you nuts? Those meant the world to
me!"

Lisa has run over, instinctively coming to
a halt a little ways away from the hole and
from Henning, as if at any moment he might
do something even crazier.

He wants to say he's sorry, to excuse himself, but can only manage a raspy croak. She
suspiciously looks him over, and suddenly
Henning realizes what she sees: not a desperate little boy, but a sweat-drenched, grown
man, panting, staring into an aljibe. As he
moves slightly toward her, she raises her
hands, warding him off.

"You'd better go now."

She runs back toward the house, across
the terrace, and into the large hall, yanking
the heavy wooden door shut behind her. It's
as if the house has closed its eyes.

The return from Femés flies by. Henning
hits the brakes a bit on each switchback, but
otherwise just lets the bike go. Seventy kilometers per hour, then eighty. His eyes water
in the headwind, he can barely see a thing,

and just focuses on steering the bike straight so it doesn't start teetering. The sheer speed swallows him up. Like a film on rewind, it erases the ascent, the strain, the struggle, the effortful sway of each pedal stroke, new year, new you. It sweeps away hunger and thirst and every last thought. The distance dissolves, the altitude dwindles. When Henning looks up and dries his eyes, he's reached Playa Blanca. As if he'd never even been so far away, but merely popped over to the bakery to pick up some fresh rolls.

At the entrance to the resort where their holiday rental is, he pauses, perching one foot on the ground. He takes out his phone and pushes a button on the side. The display lights up. The battery is at eighty-four percent. The last text message from Theresa is two days old: "Pls get yogurt+Nutella too."

In the yard, laundry flutters on a drying rack. The wind is pushing at it, but can't knock it over.

"Heya, how was it?"

Theresa steps out of the house, and the kids come running past her. "Papa, Papa, we built a castle with a moat!" They throw themselves at him, grab on to his legs, Henning opens his arms and pulls Theresa in, too. "You have a nice ride?" she mumbles, and then laughs, "Hey, not so tight!" as he hugs her close with his right arm, and Bibbi and Jonas with his left. They hug for a few moments, bound together like an eight-legged animal.

WHEN THEY GET back to Germany, laden with heavy luggage and whining kids, the stairwell smells of cigarettes.

"I thought she was just staying a couple of days," Theresa says.

Henning and Luna had agreed she'd be gone by the time he and the family came home again.

"We need the office," Theresa adds, "and I don't want her smoking up there."

"I'll go talk to her," Henning says.

Theresa picks up one of the heavy suitcases and lugs it up the stairs. She doesn't let Henning help.

Later that same evening, once the kids are in bed, Henning goes upstairs to their office and knocks on the door. Luna opens the door straightaway, lit cigarette in hand.

"Yo, Big Bro!"

She throws herself into his arms. He's happy, too—as if some doubt had arisen about whether Luna even existed. He hugs her close, then holds her back a bit and stares into her eyes. He's looking for the little girl inside. The wide eyes, round cheeks, amazed gaze. The missing incisors. But he finds only the mocking face of a strikingly pretty woman. Little Luna has vanished.

"How was vacation?"

As Henning tells her about the weather, the landscape, and the little adventures of everyday life on the island, he tidies up. He empties Luna's ashtray, makes the bed on the sleeper sofa, washes dirty dishes that have caked dry, and collects clothes strewn about the room. Luna smokes and listens. Finally he checks the fridge, finding only coffee, bread, and a few jars of tomato sauce, and plans to pick up some dark rye, fruit, and vegetables for Luna the next time he goes grocery shopping.

"Theresa doesn't want you to smoke here."

"Theresa doesn't want me to be here, with or without cigarettes."

They argue. Of course she already wanted to be long gone, but then Misha, who was going to let her crash at his place for a while, got back together with his girlfriend. And since she really doesn't like asking Rolf to stay on his couch, well, she's now looking for a more stable arrangement. And she already has a good prospect. It'll only take a couple more days, two or three, a week, tops. Henning says it's a no go. That it's high time she put out that cigarette.

"What's going on, Big Bro?"

He goes to the window and looks out. Since dusk, it has snowed again. Under the streetlights, the tops of the cars twinkle, draped in an undisturbed mantle of white. Temperatures this cold, and snow, are unusual in Göttingen. Exceptional. The news mentioned a state of emergency, with derailed trains, railroad closures, and at least one dead. Finally, Henning turns around and asks his question.

"There are photos of it," Luna replies.

And just then he realizes: the family photo album, bound in green pleather. Back when he moved out of the house he'd taken it with him, since nobody else wanted it. Now he rushes from the office and runs downstairs to their tiny basement storage space. He has to move his dust-coated bicycle aside to get to the chest full of old junk. Everything smells musty and a little mousy. Among letters, old articles for his school newspaper, and several boxes of tin soldiers, he finally finds what he's looking for. He wipes the old album off using his sleeve and carries it back upstairs, from basement to attic. Back in the office he sets it on the desk. They both lean their heads in over it.

The pages are rigid card stock interleaved with tracing paper. Henning with his goody bag on the first day of school, Luna with her gap-toothed grin. The story of her missing front teeth is a major chapter of their minor family lore, which their mother told over and over. One day during a walk in the park, little Luna was on her tricycle, and suddenly scooted straight down a hill, legs held out high, whooping and lurching, going so fast her mother couldn't catch up. The tricycle crashed into a little wall at the bottom of the hill, and Luna flew off in an arc, landing in the bushy border, but her mouth came down on a stone. Henning still remembers how proud Luna was of those missing teeth. In all the photos she has a huge grin, showing off the gaping hole.

Henning flips through the pages, the kids grow older. Luna keeps laughing by his side, pointing to a detail, saying: "Remember that?" At some point the photos come to an end, all the remaining pages are blank. As Henning goes to close the cover, a small stack of pictures falls out from the very back of the volume.

Werner sleeping on a deck chair, hair and mustache deep black, in his right hand the stub of a joint that's since gone out. Mother in sunglasses, a French braid, and a brightly colored sundress. A white Opel Corsa from the eighties, Werner at the wheel, the kids waving from the back seat. And there's the house: whitewashed walls, high ceilings, the robustly squat tower with glass dome. Palms, cacti, bougainvillea. A photo of little Henning and Luna, naked, white sun hats on their heads. They're crouching in the gravel yard and looking up at the camera.

Luna's mouth is open, her upper row of teeth is complete. And at the end Henning discovers the spiders. A close-up shot, countless, one atop the other on a white wall, forming a creepy, horrifying pattern. But it's a cool image, like something out of a nature magazine.

He drops the photo, runs to the attic window, yanks it open, and breathes the cold air in deep. The world looks transformed in this wintry costume. Luna walks over to him, wriggles under and into his arm. He holds her close as he tells the whole story. She doesn't say anything, just listens. Sometimes he feels her shivering.

When he finishes and looks at her, Luna's gazing at him with wide eyes. There she is, that little girl. She's survived in her sense of amazement.

"Can you remember any of it?" he asks.

Luna shakes her head. Of course not, she was barely two. He draws his phone from his pocket, shows her the list of received messages, and scrolls back to January 1. New Year's wishes from their mother and a few friends. Luna's own message, where she asks if she can stay at their place after the New Year, for three days max. No texts from Theresa. Henning's already checked a million times. Nothing there. Up on the mountain the strong light had been blinding, the screen had been barely visible. Henning's eyes burned, irritated by sun and wind. On top of that, there was the overexertion, exhaustion, dehydration, and hypoglycemia.

"I must've imagined the text message," Henning says, "just like all the rest of it."

"I think so, too," Luna replies. "Think about it. We were so little, no older than Bibbi and Jonas. Nobody would leave kids that young all alone."

Henning mentions how early memories are often based on photos or stories. You can even plant memories if you show adults manipulated images from their past. Then they remember things that never even happened. Luna says his subconscious must have held on to the snapshots from the photo album and then, as soon as he saw the house in Femés, built up the entire storyline. They talk for some time about the human mind, consciousness, and the question of whether reality is really more than just the sum of all the stories people continually tell themselves. A classic Henning-and-Luna discourse. When Henning returns to the apartment, Theresa is already asleep.

A few days go by. The post-vacation head colds run their course, the kids go back to nursery school, Theresa and Henning get back to work. They go grocery shopping, do the laundry, spruce up the apartment. Theresa complains about Luna still being there. Their usual daily routine returns. Even *it* makes a comeback in Henning's life. Since the holidays the attacks have gained in strength. Sometimes Henning not only thinks he's dying, he actually hopes so.

One evening he waits until the kids are in bed and Theresa is busy in the kitchen, grabs the phone, goes into the living room, and shuts the door. His mother picks up after the very first ring. She doesn't even wait for him to pose the question. She says she's been expecting his call. Ever since he'd said he was going to Lanzarote, she knew what was coming.

Henning stands by the living room couch,

staring into the black mirror of the turned-off TV screen, speechless, as she doesn't even try to dodge the issue. His mother talks on and on, enthusiastically, as if it's a relief to finally be able to talk about it.

Of course she'd promised herself time and again to address it, but ultimately she decided to leave it be. After all, nothing had really even happened. What was the gardener's name again?

"Noah," says Henning.

Yes, right, that's it! Werner was a real pothead back then. He spent half of every day with his back to them all, lounging by the side wall, and paid her little to no attention in bed. And then this half-naked, super-tan man appeared in the garden.

Henning doesn't want to hear it; at the same time, he's riveted. The vision of the hairy-backed man resurfaces in his mind, while his mother goes on to talk about their awful fight that night.

"Werner went into a rage. He said things to me that mustn't be repeated, ever. All of a sudden it wasn't just about Noah, it was about everything."

At some point Werner roared through the house, grabbed a few things, threw their wallets and his passport into a bag.

"He said he couldn't spend even one more day under the same roof as me. He planned to go to the airport and take the first flight back to Germany."

First Henning's mother tried to keep him from leaving; then she ran after the car. She couldn't just let him run away, he'd ruin everything. Ultimately it wasn't just about her, but about the kids, too. They lay peacefully in their beds. Rarely did either of them ever wake up and run to their parents' room. Certainly they wouldn't tonight, of all nights —what were the chances? She'd just go and get Werner and bring him back to his senses, they'd be back within two hours at the very most.

She remembers the steep dirt road as if it were yesterday. It wasn't completely dark out yet, but she still slipped and tripped in her sandals, fell into the dust and gravel, skinned her knuckles, and ran onward. Once he was in the rental car, Werner floored it, paying the potholes no heed, just letting the car bounce around, and then once he reached the village and the asphalt he simply roared off.

Shortly after, Henning's mother reached Femés, covered in dust and slightly limping. People were sitting outside all the houses, even kids were still playing in the streets. In front of the little grocery store she saw a young man smoking a cigarette, an old motorcycle at his side. She had a fifty-mark banknote with her, and held it right up to his face. She had to get to the airport, *aeropuerto*, now. He looked at her warily for a couple of seconds, then shrugged, yelled something back into the store, snatched the money from her, and hopped on his motorcycle. She climbed onto the back seat and held on to the young man. He kept the cigarette in the corner of his mouth until the wind nabbed it.

He leaned into the downhill curves, maybe he was enjoying driving in the arms of a foreign woman. They didn't take the steepest route toward Playa Blanca, but the somewhat gentler hills toward Arrecife. It wasn't a hefty bike, the motor hummed along at a high pitch. But it was remarkably fast. The wind flew through her hair. She thought about Werner and how she'd talk him down, how they'd drive back to the villa together in the rental car.

Just before they reached the highway to Arrecife, a car came around a sharp curve on the wrong side of the road. Maybe a drunken Brit who'd forgotten where he was. Since there was a rock face on the uphill side of the road, the young man opted for the other side. The motorcycle dove out over the scree slope, where the lava stone brought it to an abrupt halt, and Henning's mother was catapulted through the air. She made a hard landing, and everything went black.

"I first came to three days later," she says. "In a hospital on Tenerife. They airlifted me in a helicopter. There was no ICU on Lanzarote."

She had no ID on her, and nobody knew her name. No one knew where she was staying on Lanzarote, or whether she had any family members there. They'd kept her in a medically induced coma until the doctors were sure it was safe to wake her. When the police got to the villa in Femés, Henning and

Luna were gone. It didn't take long to find them. Noah had taken them home to his mother, who was looking after them.

Henning sees the house. He sees the trashed kitchen, broken glass on the floor, dried puddles of liquid, little bits of scavenged food. The master bedroom, destroyed, the bathroom with the toppled-over cabinet, the floor covered in blood. He sees Luna's shocked expression as he shoves her. Their limp bodies on the dirt road, like roadkill. He feels the impulse to apologize to his mother, and it nauseates him.

The kids were flown to Tenerife. Their mother was in no condition to travel yet, Henning and Luna slept in her hospital room, on mats right next to her bed. She said Noah did precisely the right thing. They had a lot to thank him for.

"What happened when we got back to Germany?"

"I filed for divorce."

People had long noticed this about Henning: his constant, excessive concern for Luna. Many nights he'd wake up screaming, and nothing would calm him down. Once, when he lost sight of his mother while he was playing, he suddenly flipped out. Not even her hugs could help. He screamed and screamed.

"What were you two doing at the aljibe?" his mother asks. "Apparently you were about to pry up the board covering it. I never understood what that was about."

"We wanted to free you both," Henning replies. "The monster had dragged you underground."

The silence that follows pains them both. It's time they ended the call.

"Why didn't you ever tell me?" Henning asks.

His mother audibly breathes in, and then out again.

"I thought it would be more merciful to let you forget," she says. And then she hangs up.

Henning leaves the apartment and takes the forty-two steps up to the office. Now he knows. He's traumatized, deeply traumatized, any psychologist would agree. For thirty years he's lived in an underground reservoir, in a cave, perennially anxious, taking desperate care to avoid seeing the hole he could fall into. On the first landing, he thinks everything will be different now. The knot is coming undone. Light has shone into the darkness, the monster has packed its bags and moved out. Henning will never see *it* again. He's overjoyed. He'll be free. He'll love his kids, do his work, and have regular old good and bad days. He'll only suffer all the usual things, colds, money issues, fights with his wife. Sometimes he won't be able to sleep at night, and it will mean absolutely nothing. Soon *it* will be a mere memory, he'll barely even be able to remember what it felt like, maybe he'll even think his overactive imagination magnified it all, that in reality *it* wasn't so bad after all. If he ever ends up talking about it with friends, he'll just say that the first few years with the kids were pretty rough. Hard times. But thankfully it's all over. He rode it out.

A laugh arises in his throat. He always takes two steps at a time, and virtually flies to the top floor. His heart skips a beat, then another. The first few pauses between beats are longer than they've ever been before. He grabs on to the banister, gasping for air.

Within seconds his back is drenched in sweat. He resists the urge to curl up into a ball in a corner of the stairwell. Instead, he puts one foot in front of the other. He tries to bring his breath back under control, to fully empty his lungs, in, in, out, out.

As he knocks on the door, Luna immediately opens it.

"Did you catch her?" she asks.

Henning nods.

"And?"

"It really happened," he says.

They stand facing one another. She must be able to see how he's shaking, how sweat is running down his neck. Henning looks over her head into the office behind her. It's messier than ever. Luna's things are everywhere. He closes his eyes and wants to smell her hair, but she's standing too far away. She looks like she's about to cry. He quickly steps forward and pulls her in, now she's close enough. He loves her so much it hurts, his little Luna, the most important person in the whole wide world. He wants to never let her go, hold her fast forever, meld together into a single being. He has to save her. Her and himself. And suddenly he knows how. There's only one way.

He lets go of Luna and starts picking her clothes up off the floor, stuffing them into her backpack. *It* loosens its grip. He gets her toiletries from the bathroom. He brings the backpack to the door.

"What's all this?" she asks.

"Go," he says.

They look at each other. Luna's wide-eyed, amazed gaze.

"Now," he says. "Beat it."

She obeys. Henning walks over to the window, and hears her leaving the building. He holds the windowsill tight, with both hands, to keep from running after her, from going to bring her back. The door booms shut. Luna will understand, Henning thinks, but he's not so sure he's right. His heart has calmed down, the only thing still racing is his breath. Despite the cold, it's begun snowing again. He stares into the flurry of gently falling flakes. They're wondrously slow. Down below, Luna exits the building, a grown woman. She seems like a stranger under the yellow streetlight. She looks in both directions, undecided which way she should turn. She opts for the route to the train station, where she'll blend in with the crowd. Her shadow follows her, stays back, then jumps past her like a playful dog. Her jacket's too thin, she'll catch cold. Henning opens the window, but doesn't call out to her. He lets the stench of cigarette out.

ALTA L. PRICE runs a publishing consultancy specialized in literature and nonfiction texts on art, architecture, design, and culture. A recipient of the Gutekunst Prize, she translates from Italian and German into English. Her work has appeared on BBC Radio 4, *3 Quarks Daily*, *Words Without Borders*, and elsewhere. Her latest publications include books by Martin Mosebach, Dana Grigorcea, Anna Goldenberg, and Alexander Kluge.

On the Design

As book design is an integral part of the reading experience, we would like to acknowledge the work of those who shaped the form in which the story is housed.

Tessa van der Waals (Netherlands) is responsible for the cover design, cover typography, and art direction of all World Editions books. She works in the internationally renowned tradition of Dutch Design. Her bright and powerful visual aesthetic maintains a harmony between image and typography and captures the unique atmosphere of each book. She works closely with internationally celebrated photographers, artists, and letter designers. Her work has frequently been awarded prizes for Best Dutch Book Design.

The arresting, sharp font on the front cover is YWFT Jute. Our designer Tessa van der Waals chose the stark black background to reflect both the dark aspect of the story and the festive night sky of New Year's Eve. The title is written in typical firework colors, with fireworks shooting out of the top of the *Y*.